The Flight of Time

Susan Connelly

iUniverse, Inc.
Bloomington

The Flight of Time

iUniverse books may be ordered through booksellers or by contacting:

iUniverse
1663 Liberty Drive
Bloomington, IN 47403
www.iuniverse.com
1-800-Authors (1-800-288-4677)

Author photo credit: Photography © Annie Higbee/ Imagewright

ISBN: 978-1-4759-3487-8 (sc)
ISBN: 978-1-4759-3488-5 (e)

Printed in the United States of America

iUniverse rev. date: 6/26/2012

In memory of Marilyn Haines

ACKNOWLEDGMENTS

Editor, Patty Lane, the sharpest eye

First reader, Peggy Emanuel, my cheering section

My catalog of heroes, from home and away,
for your thousand kindnesses

Exegi monumentum aere perennius…
quod non imber edax, non Aquilo impotens
possit diruere aut innumerabilis
annorum series et fuga temporum.

(I have erected a monument more lasting than bronze. The violent North Wind, the numberless run of the years, the flight of time cannot destroy it.)

Horace. Odes III. 30

CHAPTER ONE

might have had trouble recognizing Terry Burke if I wasn't expecting her. When she called on a warm Monday at the end of April to ask if she could come to my office, my immediate response had been, "Office nothing, lady. If work and motherhood are simultaneously giving you time off, I am taking you somewhere very swanky for lunch."

Terry, who loves food, turned that offer down flat and said she needed to see me at my office. I gave her my first appointment for the following day and hung up with a feeling of unease.

Now, setting out raspberry scones to go with the coffee perking on my credenza, I thought of what Terry had done for me and was glad that, whatever it was she needed, she had come to me. I had asked on the phone if anything was wrong with her family and Terry said no, but her tone was at odds with her words. I was glad she was my first appointment, because I probably wouldn't have been able to concentrate on other things until I knew what her trouble was.

There was a knock on the door. Knowing that Terry must have a problem serious enough for her to need a private investigator, I refrained from more of the happy reaction I'd felt when she called. But I did swing open the door with more enthusiasm than I would for most clients.

" Terry!" I said. "And then, "Terry...?"

"That bad?" she said, and I rapidly shook my head. *Sorry. No. Of course not.* Terry stepped inside and I reached to close the door behind her. I wanted to hug her, but she had her head down and was unzipping a black nylon jacket. A jacket in this heat? And black—where had her love of bold colors and flamboyant style gone? When had she gotten her thick auburn hair cut short?

1

"Emmy's coat," Terry said. "Miss Goth, at eleven years old. I just helped myself from her closet. Or I should say from the floor of her closet."

This was more like the old Terry and I started to smile, but was struck by a question more serious and worrying than the others that had occurred to me. Since when did Terry Burke, whose voluptuous full figure made her beautiful rather than pretty, fit into an eleven-year-old's clothes?

"She's all self-conscious about the way she's starting to develop," Terry said, as if I had spoken aloud. "So everything has to be big and baggy. Plus"—she pulled her arms out of the sleeves and let the jacket drop—"There's the new me."

The new Terry was at least twenty pounds thinner than the lady I'd known. It wasn't an improvement—there was a looseness to her skin, especially in her face, which had been round and full and always smiling. I said, "You look great. Not that there was a thing wrong with the old you. But you know me—old is good."

Terry did in fact know about my passion for the ancient classical world. I had been reading Herodotus last year when a question came to me that I called her about—her answer ended up cracking my case. When I later told her exactly what the association had been, she listened patiently while I went on about the Athenians and the Spartans and the original Marathoner, Pheidippides. Finally, she patted my arm and said, "Honey. You found the baby, but you've sure lost me."

Now, seeing the changes in my friend, I thought of the circumstances that had first brought us together. Terry is Director of Human Resources at Higgins and Lathrop, one of Boston's largest investment firms. A year and a half ago she helped me in every way possible to solve a case and bring an abducted baby safely home. In her private life she's married and the mother of a son and two daughters, whom she sighs over dramatically at every opportunity while deceiving no one about her real feelings for her children.

I said to Terry, "I apologize for the air conditioning, or lack of it. The landlord is supposed to be sending someone by to look at it, but if he actually shows up I'll send him away until you and I are finished." May was still a week away, but Boston was suffering under a heat wave that had the hardware stores running out of fans and an increasing number of people deciding that Al Gore might be right. There was very little chance the repairman—my landlord's cousin, whose working papers were probably not in the best order—would choose today to actually appear, and if he did I'd just wait a little longer for refrigerated air.

"Terry, before I get us coffee I need to know something. Are any of you sick? You or Russ, the kids?"

"No," she said. "It's nothing like that."

"Good. Tell me what you take in your coffee and then we'll talk about what's worrying you."

I doubled up on the cream and sugar she asked for and put two scones on the napkin I'd laid in front of her on my desk. We sipped at our coffee while I waited for her to find an opening. It came when she commented on my bulletin board, which held several small photographs and one large one.

"Who's the good-looking boy?"

"That's Luke. My nephew. He's sixteen."

"You never said you had a nephew."

"A long story, which I shall tell you one of these days over the aforementioned swanky lunch. At which time I will also beg you for the secret to raising a kid and keeping your sanity all at the same time." I touched her hand. "For now—your turn."

She set her cup on the desk. "It's Russ," she said, then turned to look at me. "Nell, I'm so worried…"

CHAPTER TWO

"From the beginning," I said. "Just talk. Do you want more coffee?"

She shook her head. I saw that the mug she had her right hand around was still full. She hadn't touched the pastries, either. "Come on," I said. "Let's sit on the couch." She looked over at the piece of furniture I was referring to—a blueberry colored tweed item I had taken in trade from a furniture dealer who, citing seasonal cash flow problems, had been unable to come up with the fee for a job I'd done for him. The couch was long enough for me to stretch out on if I felt the need for a break, and accepting it, garish color and all, beat suing my own client in small claims court.

"I had hopes of seducing handsome male clients on it," I told Terry, "but business has been slow. You can be my first customer—I promise to keep my hands to myself."

I had hoped to make her smile, and she did try, but the expression of strain and sadness on her face didn't change. I put a hand on her shoulder.

"Come on. We'll figure it out together."

I had met Terry's husband just once, when she invited me to dinner at their house. We were celebrating the safe return of the baby, Andrea Reed, whose father had been so driven by financial desperation that he'd faked a kidnapping of his own daughter. Russ was a quiet guy, friendly but reserved, though the reserve may have come from being surrounded by his voluble wife and three excited kids tearing at the wrappings of the presents I'd brought them. "What do you say?" Terry had prompted before the children had even seen what, with advice from experts, I'd gotten them. "Show Ms. Prentice that I've brought you hooligans up right." There was a chorus of thank-yous, to which Terry added, "And Mommy and Daddy thank you for this lovely bottle of wine, which we are going to start on this very minute."

Russ went to look for a corkscrew. ("It's in the junk drawer, honey," Terry called to him. "No—the other junk drawer. Annabelle, put that bubble wrap in the recycling basket. You remember the time the dog chewed a piece and had to go to the vet...") Under cover of her husband's absence and the kids' noise I had asked Terry, "How are all of you readjusting?"

Terry took my question seriously enough to give it some thought before answering. "Adjustment is the word for it," she said finally. "When his unit of the Guard was sent to Iraq, I'd just think that if he came home safe we'd be the happiest family ever. But the kids got used to getting around me without him here—especially Matthew. We had to establish some new rules once Daddy came back." She gave me her grin that was one of the first things I'd noticed about her. "I did tell Russ that if he ever left again I'd mail him the kids and run off with Brad Pitt. What? Are you implying that he wouldn't dump Angelina for me the second he had a chance?"

"He'd definitely be trading up," I said. "So all in all, things are good?"

"Yes," she had said, smiling. "Things are good, Nell."

Sitting in my office now, Terry said, " It was natural for me to worry about him when he was in Iraq. But now that there's almost no chance of his getting shot at or blown up, I worry about his work at the VA hospital. He takes it so seriously—staying strong for the patients, whether it's their bodies or their minds that got hurt. Then coming home and playing with the kids, acting silly with them no matter what his day's been like."

I said, "Do you know of anything specific going on at work for him?"

"That's just it, Nell. He's left his job."

CHAPTER THREE

I knew Terry was going to tell me her story—it was why she'd come, after all. But before I let her get started I said, "Terry, you've got three kids and who knows how many dogs and cats and fish. I only know about the pet food part—oh, right, and my nephew's teenaged appetite— but feeding a houseful must get expensive. Are you OK for money?"

"You forgot Jeremiah," Terry said. "Matthew's hamster." She smiled then, and I had a glimpse of the old Terry, the one whose biggest worry was the cost of kids' shoes. "We're good on that score, Nell, thanks to you. You're the one who told Mr. Martin the reward money should go to me. He was actually suspicious at first—like I might have known something about where the baby was and didn't say anything. But then after I got the reward a raise came through, too. All your doing."

"You deserved that money," I said. "As for Edward Martin, he might not have seen his granddaughter again if it weren't for you remembering about Dee."

"Well," Terry said, "I think what convinced him was when I couldn't even pronounce that guy's name you told me about. Phi...Phip..."

"Pheidippides," I said. "Maybe you don't have spare time to live in the past the way I do, what with raising a family and going to work and worrying about your husband. But that's what did it, Terry. I was reading about the run from Marathon to Sparta, and then you remembered hearing Vince D'Angelo's nickname when he ran in Boston."

"I was thinking of him a couple of weeks ago," Terry said. "Because of the Marathon. I can't help feeling sorry for all of them, even though what they did was so stupid and the baby could have gotten hurt."

'All of them' were Vince D'Angelo, his childless sister and brother-in-law, and Daniel Reed, father of the missing baby. I couldn't share Terry's magnanimity of spirit toward those four people—whatever their motives, they had put an innocent child at risk—but this was not the time to express my contrary view. I said, "If it weren't for you, Andrea's mother might not be planning her daughter's fourth birthday party next week. But I want to hear about you. You said Russ quit his job..."

She nodded. I still wasn't used to her short hair and expected to see it bouncing up and down when she moved her head. "Yes," she said. "Over one of his cases."

"A disagreement over treatment? Something like that?"

"No. There was always plenty of that, though. Russ takes all his cases so much to heart. He gets unbelievably frustrated when the same government that sends these people to war won't pay for what they need when they come home. Russ says it's hard enough for veterans to admit they're having emotional problems, then to have to fight to get treatment..."

"And that's what was happening?"

"Yes. Nell—promise me you won't take this the wrong way, but is this confidential?"

A very reasonable question. I patted her hand and got up from the sofa to go to my desk. From the right-hand drawer I took out a standard contract, which I held up.

"This piece of paper, along with a dollar from you, makes you my client." I saw she was about to say something, possibly about the modest amount of the retainer. "The dollar makes it legal. Once I've received consideration from you, anything you tell me is protected by client privilege."

"It's not that I think you'd repeat anything..."

"I understand that," I said. "But this is still the best way. So cough up a buck—I even take loose change."

Terry got up and went to the chair where she'd left her purse. Out came tissues, a juice box, colored pens, and finally her wallet. I took the dollar she handed me and insisted she read the contract before she signed it. I added my own signature, put the contract and the dollar in my desk, and took a pen and notebook back to the sofa.

"I'm ready. About Russ's case?"

As she sat back down next to me Terry nudged a scone on the plate, then didn't take it. "I'm sorry," she said. "I shouldn't be touching things if I'm not going to eat them. I always tell the kids…"

"Terry," I said. "Forget about the scone. Forget about your kids' manners, which I'm sure are excellent. What happened with Russ's patient?"

"Russ would approve," Terry said, and for a moment I thought her remark was more stalling. "He never calls patients 'cases,' and I shouldn't either. He's even gotten in trouble a few times for insisting on reminding the higher-ups that these are people—they have names."

"And can you tell me the name of the person Russ was counseling?"

Terry nodded. "If I weren't too upset to be thinking straight I'd never have gone into all that stuff about confidentiality. What does it matter now? Russ knows he's supposed to stay objective, but he tells me some of these guys need a friend just as much as they need medications and physical therapy. Oliver became a special friend—he came to the house a few times, the kids really took to him. Now he's dead, and Russ blames himself."

Terry had tears in her eyes, and I got up to fetch the box of tissues I keep on my desk. She wiped her eyes and looked around for a place to put the tissue. "Just leave it," I said. "I want to hear about Oliver. Was he married?"

Terry shook her head. "After Russ brought him home a few times and I saw how good he was with the kids, I used to tease him about it. What was a catch like him doing hanging around with dull old married people when he could be making some girl very happy? He said…" Terry swallowed, and wiped again at her eyes with the tissue she was still holding. "He said there was plenty of time for that."

"How old was he?" I asked, very businesslike, even as I felt a lump in my own throat for someone I had never met.

"Twenty-five. But he had this baby face—he looked like a kid himself when he'd be swinging Matthew around or listening to Emmy talk about school. Poor Emmy," Terry said, giving her head a slight, sympathetic shake. "People don't remember how those first crushes can break a little girl's heart."

"So he didn't have a girlfriend?"

"I'm pretty sure he didn't. He knew if he did she'd be welcome at our house. Well, maybe not by Emmy. He was staying with his mother since he got back from Iraq, working as a bank trainee, but what he really wanted was to be a chef."

"It sounds as if he talked a lot to you."

"Oh, he did. I hope he knew how much we all…loved him."

"Terry," I said, "You're one of those people. It really comes across when you care about someone. I'm sure he knew."

"Thank you," she said, so softly that I missed all over again the bubbly extrovert I had first met. Then, "His mother called us herself. I guess Oliver had talked to her about Russ and all of us and where we lived. She got our number out of the phone book. Emmy answered and told Russ there was a lady crying on the phone. When Russ picked up she told him she was Oliver's mother and that he…he was dead." Terry began to cry again and I moved closer to wrap an arm around her as she choked out the rest of it. "He slit his wrists."

"Oh, Terry," I said, and hugged her to me, feeling the change in her body that grief had made. She cried quietly for another minute, her tears falling on the plain maroon top she was wearing, then she reached for the tissue box.

"You're going to be in the poorhouse if I keep using up your tissues like this," she snuffled.

"They're tax-deductible," I said, thinking that if they weren't they should be. My choice of profession means that I spend most days listening to people's sorrows. "Would it make things easier if I asked you questions?"

"Yes," she said. "I bet you never thought you'd see the day when you had to beg me to talk."

She seemed to be trying to lighten the atmosphere in my office with her remark, which I rewarded with a much bigger smile than it may have warranted. "That's the spirit," I said. "I suppose there's nothing to lose by making the first question the big one. Why would Russ blame himself for what happened?"

Terry drew in a congested-sounding breath and let it out. "I've asked myself that ever since this happened. I've asked *him*. All he keeps saying is that it's his job to notice when people might be planning something. He says he failed Oliver as his counselor *and* his friend—that he's no good to anyone at the hospital if he's going to miss warning signs."

"Maybe there weren't any," I said. "People who are in a dark place and don't want their friends to know it can get pretty good at hiding what they're going through."

"That's it exactly!" Terry said. "Oh, Nell—will you talk to him? The hospital hasn't even accepted his resignation—they're calling it a leave of absence and saying they want him back, but I don't know how long they can keep the job open…"

"Of course I'll talk to him," I said. "Terry, here's what I want you to do. Go home and tell Russ you've been to see me, because you're worried about him. Give him ten minutes or so to vent about how it's a private thing and then tell him that I'm your friend and his friend, and that means we look out for each other. Tell him I want him to explain to me exactly why he feels responsible for this and if he won't…"—I paused, waiting for some dire consequence to strike my imagination—"…then I'll sit outside his window all night and recite Aeschylus at the top of my lungs."

Terry laughed—a wonderful sight and sound. To hear more of it I added, "And if that doesn't work I'll be forced to resort to my top professional skill. Making an ungodly nuisance of myself until I get my way."

"Oh, Nell," Terry said. "My kids are great at that. Who knew they could make a living that way?" She reached for her purse and said, "I'm going home right now and tell him just what you said. But first we have to settle on what I owe you."

I put up a hand to forestall her opening the purse. "I'm in uncharted territory here, Terry. Until we have some idea whether I can help, that dollar you gave me is just fine."

Terry got up from the sofa. "It was a lucky day when I met you, Nell."

I stood and hugged her. "Meant to be, some of my favorite philosophers would say. Do you want to take the scones?"

"No, thanks. Well—maybe just the one I touched." She looked doubtfully at the plate, and I laughed.

"There's really no need for you to worry on that score," I said. "The pigeons on the Boston Common are notoriously unfussy."

CHAPTER FOUR

had told Terry I had lots of time to live in the past, but that's not nearly as true now as it was eighteen months earlier when she and I first met. In that short time my friendship with my dear Martha has deepened and I've acquired a nephew I love pretty much all the time. I've laid some ghosts to rest, and fallen in love again.

I dialed the Newton Police Station. "Hi, Naomi," I said, familiar now with the people my man worked with. "It's Nell. Is Tom in?"

"Oh, hi, Nell," she said. "In his office. The man starts his paperwork eleven minutes after he gets back from a scene—I wish we could clone him. Tom…" she must have pushed a line button. "It's your… well, I'll let you be surprised."

I began to regret my impulse, hoping I wasn't embarrassing Tom by calling him at work, but was reassured when he came on the line sounding happy to hear from me. "Hey, beautiful. In need of a hard working officer of the law?"

"It happens that I am. So much so that I am willing to cook dinner, share my cat, give up for the evening my affair with Herodotus, et cetera."

"What's on the menu?"

I hadn't actually thought that far ahead. "It's hot," I said. "Maybe I'll fling together a chef's salad for us."

"I'll bring wine," Tom said. "I can't wait to see what the et cetera is."

The success of my impulsive call put me in a much better frame of mind than I'd been in when Terry left. My IN basket held a pile of receipts, papers, and parking stubs—no two the same size (why is that?)—which I sorted for filing with the proper accounts. My volume of work is not steady enough to justify hiring a secretary, but I'm a Taurus, and most of us find this kind of organizing work quite satisfying. When the basket was empty I dusted it with a paper towel and made phone calls and did billing before going to lunch at Burger King. I had a twinge of guilt at my restaurant choice—Tom was still on a very restricted diet since his heart attack back in October—but I quelled the twinge by having the smaller size of French fries with my double cheeseburger. Then I worked until three and gave myself permission to go home early. The landlord's cousin never had shown up to check the air conditioning, my irate calls to the landlord himself were stacking up in his voice mail, and I really needed a shower and a change of clothes before Tom arrived.

At the supermarket I picked up the ingredients for a chef's salad, choosing turkey instead of ham, reduced fat cheese, and foregoing the eggs. Tom's enforced regimen was having a good influence on my own eating habits, except when I was lured off course by the Siren song of Burger King. I added French bread and pseudo butter to my basket and, even though my kitchen cabinet was filled with assorted cat treats, a new flavor called Toothsome Tuna.

"Woody, I'm home," I called, opening the door to my apartment just enough to slip my recyclable grocery bag inside. With Woody distracted by the food smells coming from the bag I got quickly inside and closed the door behind me. My cat left his sniffing to come rub against my leg and I reached down to pet him. "Pretty boy," I said. "In a minute I have treats for you."

I put the salad materials in the refrigerator and went to have my shower. When I came out I opened the cat treats and tossed Woody one to sample. He liked it just fine, so I tossed him several more before putting the package in the cabinet with a half dozen others, all opened. With people food my rule is to finish one variety or choice before opening another, but such rules go out the window where my cat is concerned.

"Tom's on his way," I told Woody. "You look fine, but I need to get presentable."

I toweled my hair dry and put on jeans and a lavender top Tom liked. The top was pretty but too casual for me to wear my Christmas present from Tom with it. I opened my jewelry box and took out the pendant he'd given me—a depiction of Athena worked in delicate silver. As I held the beautiful necklace I remembered that it had crossed my mind that the jewelry box might contain a ring, and that my thoughts about such a possibility had been decidedly ambivalent. What would my reaction be now if Tom were to ask me...

There was a knock on the door. Woody's tail shot up and he ran to welcome whoever was out there. "Tom?" I called. "Just let me get Woody..."

I picked up my cat and held him in my left arm as I undid the door locks. As soon as Tom was inside I put Woody down so I could kiss Tom. Woody, never the jealous type, circled us, purring.

"You look pretty," Tom said, which was more than enough incentive for me to kiss him again. With my arms wrapped around him I said, "I was just looking at the beautiful pendant my guy gave me. I'm afraid all I have to offer him at the moment is a beer."

"Light, I suppose," Tom said, grimacing.

"To borrow from Virgil, light as air. But so you won't feel deprived, we'll save this wine you've bought and I shall partake of nothing stronger than iced tea."

We sat on the sofa, sipping our drinks and giving Woody lots of attention. On my part, this was somewhat motivated by guilt, since if all went well Woody would be the only one in the house sleeping alone tonight. Tom asked about my nephew Luke, who would be out of school for the summer in a few weeks.

"He's doing well," I said. "We tend to communicate best by email. When we're on the phone or together I don't get much out of him."

"It's the age," Tom said. "Will he come here for the summer?"

If Luke did stay with me during his school vacation, Tom and I wouldn't have the privacy and freedom we took for granted. But I knew Tom well enough to be fairly certain that wasn't his first consideration.

"He'll be here for a few days," I said, "before I drive him to Maine. He wants to be with his buddy Zach. And Miles and Tilda, God bless them, for some reason they're eager to have two teenaged boys instead of just one."

"Good people," Tom said. "I hope I get to see them again. Not this time," he added quickly. "You and Luke should have this trip to yourselves. But while he's here I'd like to take him to Fenway if he's interested."

I put my glass on the coffee table and reached across Woody to squeeze Tom's hand. "Woody already wants to follow you home—my nephew will be right behind him."

"Speaking of home," Tom said, "My mother's been dropping pretty heavy hints that you and I don't need two apartments. This from a nice Catholic girl."

"Well," I said, getting up and peering toward the kitchen as if tossing a salad was going to require complex culinary skills, "I guess times have changed."

As an evasion that was pretty feeble, but it was enough to get me unchallenged into the kitchen, where I filled Woody's dish and put Tom's and my dinner on the table. The salad, healthy dressing and all, was tasty, and there was just enough left over for me to decide I'd take it to the office tomorrow and pass on the red meat for lunch. I loaded the dishwasher, poured more iced tea for both of us, and sat back down at the table across from Tom.

"I saw Terry Burke today," I said. "She came to my office."

"On business?"

I nodded. "She's lost weight. And her husband's quit his job."

I told Tom the basic facts of Russ and Terry's situation, feeling I was on the right side of the client confidentiality line. I was sharing what Terry had told me with a trustworthy friend who might be able to offer some valuable insights. When I had finished Tom said, "I admire anybody who can do that kind of work. Counseling guys coming back from a war zone. That's one thing that's changed for the better—in my Dad's day veterans didn't talk about what they'd seen."

I said, "I told Terry I really didn't know if I could help. But I owe it to her to try."

"Well," Tom said, "Count me in if there's anything I can help with." He grinned suddenly. "Would I be right or wrong in thinking that Terry is getting a discount on your fee?"

"I charged her a dollar. Until I know whether I can actually do anything."

"Damn. And I was planning to marry you for your money."

The M word. Not money—marry. I said, "I'm banking on karma. Maybe if I can be a friend to Terry, the investigator gods will send me a paying case."

Our glasses were empty. When I reached across the table to take Tom's glass, he caught my hand and kissed it. I drew in my breath.

"The weather guy says it's going to be a warm night. Fortunately, there's an air conditioner in my bedroom."

CHAPTER FIVE

I woke up to find myself alone in bed, but with the spot next to me still warm. "Tom," I called, rubbing my eyes.

"Out here. I'm making coffee."

"Maybe I will marr..."

There was a silence. Then Tom stuck his head in the doorway. He was grinning.

"That's all it would take? I should have mastered the art of opening a coffee can sooner."

"That's not what I started to say." The moment the lie had passed the barriers of my teeth I realized I was caught. What started out sounding like "marry," but wasn't? Maroon? Marinate? Reluctantly, I altered the quantity of the vowel.

"I was going to say "marvel." I'll marvel at your domestic skills as soon as I'm fully awake."

"Right," Tom said. "Shall I feed Woody?"

"Now you're trying to enlist my own cat as an ally. Yes, please—just give him half a can no matter how much he sucks in his cheeks to look underfed." He turned from the doorway and I said, "Tom..."

"Call me back one more time and I'm going to forget about the coffee and come back to bed."

"I wish. The thing is, if I'm late to my office there's nobody to notice. If you are, we'll both hear about it."

"Sometimes I think Naomi is actually calling my mother to report developments. What did you want?"

"Use the coffee in the green can. The decaffeinated."

We ate at the kitchen counter, with sun pouring in and the radio playing quietly. Woody was in the window cleaning his face and paws after his breakfast. The weatherman said the heat had broken late the previous night and that today's temperatures would be in the seasonable low fifties. I picked out a skirt and top, added a sweater just in case the air conditioner magician actually showed up and got my "unit" working again, and kissed Tom goodbye as he left for his own place before going on to work. He said, "I'll keep my fingers crossed that karma thing comes through for you."

"Thank you. Have a good day at work. I'll call you tonight."

The morning was beautiful, so much so that I got off the train a few stops early and walked to my office, stopping to pick up a large cup of real coffee and a croissant. After all, I was having a salad for lunch, which as everyone knows is negative calories. I was at my desk virtually swooning from my jolt of caffeine when the phone rang. Karma, so soon?

"Nell Prentice Investigating," I said, quickly swallowing a bite of pastry. "This is Nell Prentice."

"Nell, it's Martha."

Not a potentially lucrative case, then, but a very fine way to begin my day—hearing from my old friend who had gotten me through the bad times just after my husband Michael died.

"I won't keep you," Martha was saying. "I know you're at work. I was just calling to ask if you and Tom can come here on Sunday for your birthday."

"That sounds great," I said. "I'll ask him tonight and let you know."

"Wonderful. I'll make whatever you want. And a cake, of course. And Nell…"

I was already in a daydream of cheeseburgers grilled out on Martha's deck, her red bliss potato salad, maybe some red wine, but collected myself sufficiently to respond with "Yes?"

"Tell Tom to call me. I might have some ideas what he could get you for your birthday."

I hung up the phone and thought that the birthday Martha was referring to—my forty-third, a week away—was not going to be quite so simple as my forty-second. Last year, I had stopped by Laura Reed's house with a present for her daughter Andy, turning three the day after my own birthday, enjoyed a piece of Little Mermaid cake, and then driven to Manomet to have dinner at Martha's. Those juicy cheeseburgers, eaten at the kitchen table instead of on the deck because it was raining. This year, with Tom's low-fat diet, I'd have to ask Martha to grill chicken instead, with a salad. Iced tea instead of wine. And then there was Luke—would he think he was supposed to get his Aunt Nell a present? Would he feel he had to spend a lot, as I had for the leather jacket he'd wanted when he turned sixteen (at least he hadn't asked for a car) and which I managed to refrain from telling him made him look like a movie star. Would Martha steer Tom toward some sexy unmentionables for me instead of the new translation of *Lysistrata* I coveted?

Well, poor you, I told myself. Three generations of people you love picking out presents they think you'll like. Martha's great cooking, and Tom there, too. And the last I heard you have a few dollars saved—if you want Aristophanes' take on what might really end war once and for all, you can just get yourself to a bookstore and buy the book yourself.

Maybe as soon as that paying case materializes.

CHAPTER SIX

Sunday was cool and sunny, a fine May Day, with forsythia and lilac in bud. Woody had wanted to come along on the car trip, of course, but Martha has a cat, Iris, who is very proprietary about who can and cannot enter her domain, and who is especially opinionated on whether any cat other than her may climb into Martha's lap. Not wanting to see my sweet boy rejected by anybody, I made sure he had extra cat treats and told him I wouldn't be late and would bring him some chicken.

Tom was waiting for me in front of his apartment building. As he came toward my car I noticed an envelope sticking out of his shirt pocket.

"This is for you," he said, tapping the envelope as he got into the car. "But you're going to have to wait until we're at Martha's—her present and mine go together. She's been emailing Luke, too, so you can expect something from him in the mail."

"In cahoots, the whole lot of you," I said. "I hope Martha told Luke not to spend too much. And the same goes for both of you. My family is made up of a lady in her eighties of modest means, a schoolboy, and a brilliant police detective who, sadly, is not paid a fraction of what he's worth."

"It's amazing we managed a phone call and a few emails without you," Tom said. "As for any financial strain on Luke, it's my understanding that Martha is 'helping' with that part of it. He'll come out ahead of the game and probably wish his aunt had more than one birthday a year."

"But..."

"Nell." Tom touched my arm, bare in the summer dress the weather was not quite warm enough for. He left his hand there, and I felt the hairs rise. "We want to do this. It's not a big deal. We think you're special—I think you're special—and we want to show it on your birthday."

I looked at his hand on my arm, then at him. "It's having you in my life that's a big deal. But you're going to have to put your hand back where it belongs if you don't want me to start looking for a motel."

A half hour later we were knocking on Martha's door. She opened it smiling, then beamed as she saw that Tom and I were holding hands.

"Look at you two. Tom, how are you?" She kissed him, then me as I let go of Tom's hand to hug her. I saw her glance at the envelope in Tom's pocket. He nodded, and I felt a lump in my throat at their conspiracy to make me happy.

"I'm the only one here in the dark about that mysterious envelope," I said. "I bet even Iris knows what the two of you have cooked up."

"Iris," Martha called, "Can you come greet our guests?"

Woody would have been prancing with excitement at the door the minute he heard a car, but Iris was named—by Luke—for a goddess, and conducted herself accordingly. When no cat appeared Martha said, "She expects us to come to her. Her favorite spot to hold court is my kitchen window."

The table in Martha's sunny kitchen was set for three, and there was Iris, in a spot that had held plants before she moved in and arranged everything to her liking. She turned her face to us—she had a spark shape on her forehead, with two graceful lines trailing from it. Tom smiled at her, and the cat blinked once. He could stay.

"Hello, Iris," I said. "Have you been taking good care of Martha?"

Iris regarded me steadily. A trivial remark, and therefore beneath her notice. She looked away from me, yawned, and closed her eyes.

"Oh, dear," Martha said, laughing. "I apologize for her manners."

"She's reminding us of what Henry V says to his Queen," I said. Tom and Martha both looked at me. At least they didn't yawn.

" 'We are the makers of manners,' " I quoted. "Iris is royalty. If mere mortals are not amusing or admiring her she's not interested. After all, you wouldn't expect Cleopatra to make small talk with you on the deck of her barge."

Tom said, "I saw that movie. It came around again for, I think it was its tenth anniversary. I went with—"

I knew, from the abrupt way he stopped himself. It wasn't that he was self-conscious about mentioning a date he'd been on long before we ever met—it had to be that he'd seen the movie with Mary Alice Herlihy.

I have a deep core of privacy myself, and am equally protective of the privacy of the people I care about. I had never told Martha anything about the girl Tom had planned to marry and spend his life with. The girl who told him he'd have to give up the work that was so much a part of who he was, settle for something without the kind of risk that had taken his partner's life. I thought now that if he'd been a man who could accept such a choice, I might have passed him in the street with his red-headed kids instead of having him here right beside me, in Martha's house.

It was obvious Martha had noticed Tom's uncompleted sentence, but she said nothing. Discretion is one of her many virtues. She said, "Let me serve our lunch, so you can see that at least one person living here knows how to treat guests. Please sit where you like at the table."

Tom held my chair, and I thanked him as he took the chair opposite me. I knew he'd get up again when Martha, taking chicken smelling of rosemary from the oven, came to the table. The aroma of the food caused Iris to sniff the air, but she was too dignified to show any overt interest, much less beg like the disguised Odysseus the way Woody was wont to do.

Martha put the chicken on a platter and set it on the table next to a brown loaf of bread and a bowl of salad. As Tom stood and held her chair I tried to see if his face had cleared of the strain I'd seen when he started to tell us about his date to see *Cleopatra*, and remembered whatever he had remembered. He sounded fine, telling Martha how good everything looked, and I relaxed and set myself to enjoying a good meal with the best of friends. As Martha passed me the salad I had one last image of the Queen of the Nile. Not from the fascinating stories of her love affairs with the world's most powerful men, or the unimaginable opulence of her court, or even the sinister asp that harbored her death in its lethal fangs. I was seeing not the figures of legend but a real man and a real woman, twenty centuries gone. Mark Antony watching transfixed from the prow of his ship in the Bay of Actium as his lover Cleopatra turned her painted fleet and, her purple sail growing ever smaller, abandoned the battle and sailed for home.

Martha said there was cake "of course" but that perhaps we could have it after I got to see what she and Tom had for me. I had seen Tom give her his envelope when we came into the house—she put it on a small table I remembered from her husband Ben's study in Newton. She left Tom and me sitting on the sofa and returned with two envelopes, one flat and one rounded with its contents.

"Just like the Oscars," I said.

"Oh, it is," Martha agreed, sounding pleased. "In the Best Detective category...Oh, that will never work." She giggled, and covered her mouth. "You're both detectives..."

"They have male and female categories," I said. "May I please, please see what's in those envelopes?"

Martha handed the flat envelope not to me but to Tom. Taking it, he said to me, "Martha was telling me that when you stay here she likes to go past the guest room and see you reading in the rocking chair, with an afghan around you." He passed the envelope to me, and I opened it and took out a folded page printed off a website.

"Shaker Workshops has one just like it," Tom said, touching the illustration on the page I had unfolded. "You could decide just what you'd like and I'll put it together for you and finish it and weave the seat."

I met his eyes. "What a lovely idea."

"Martha thought of it," Tom said. "And I really like to do woodworking. I should warn you, though—I'm a slow craftsman. If you agree to this, you're going to have me around for quite a while."

"You can unweave the tape by night," I said, still looking at him. "You can work on it until I'm old and creaky and need a rocking chair full time."

"*I'm* still a long way from that," Martha said. "And while Tom is meticulously fashioning you a rocking chair—" She held out the rounded envelope, and I saw that it was filled with short strands of yarn, in every imaginable color.

"...I will make you an afghan. You and Woody can snuggle in the chair together under an afghan in whatever colors you like, and feel that you're here."

22

"And so I shall," I said. "Thank you. Thank you both. This is… inspired." I kissed first Martha, then Tom, before fingering through the colored yarns. "Maybe I'll choose the colors of Iris's rainbow."

"Iris," Martha said. "I promised that lady some chicken. I'll wrap some up for Woody, too, and then I'll bring in the cake."

An hour later, as Tom and I gathered our things, I put the two envelopes in my purse and thought of what a wealth of love they contained. Tom had the leftover chicken and cake, so it wasn't the smell of food that motivated Iris, most unexpectedly, to stand up against me and bump my hand with her head.

"Why, Iris," I said, "Thank you. To what do I owe this honor? Are you wishing me a happy birthday?" Even this witless remark did not deter Martha's standoffish cat, who continued to nuzzle me and even began to purr. I was still talking about it after Tom and I had said our goodbyes and I was starting the car.

"Did you see how Iris liked me? She doesn't take to very many people at all. But there she was, acting all affectionate just like Woody does, and did you hear her purring…?"

Tom finished fastening his seatbelt and grinned at me.

"Iris," he said, "is a lady who understands all about playing hard to get."

We left Manomet in a Spring twilight, the roads free of the summer traffic that would invade the Cape in just a few weeks. As we got back onto Route 3 Tom asked, "Do you want to stop for dinner?"

I'd had two slices of Martha's chocolate cake, with ice cream, which should tide me over until we reached Boston. I looked at Tom, thinking of how he would look in his denim shirt, working on my present. "Do you mind if we don't? Woody's been alone all day, and I've got soup I could heat up for us." I smiled at him. "Come home with me."

CHAPTER SEVEN

The day before I turned forty-three, karma delivered my paying case.

The cool weekend weather had departed, the heat and humidity were back with a vengeance, and the air conditioner still wasn't fixed. I called the landlord as soon as I arrived in my office, listened to his feigned dismay that his kinsman hadn't been Johnny-on-the-spot to restore what I was, after all, paying for, and received his fervent assurance that his cousin would be at the door of my steamy premises within the hour. When I hung up, I saw that a call had gone to voice mail while the landlord and I engaged in our charade. I pressed the Play button.

"Ms. Prentice? This is Alice Kent at Hathorne College. I'm calling for Dr. Alec Benson. Dr. Benson is hoping to speak to you in your professional capacity. Could you please call me at this number…"

Dr. Alec Benson. Renowned classicist and authority on Hesiod. Like some Bronze Age groupie I fumbled dialing the number I'd been given and had to do it a second time, but at least by the time Ms. Kent answered I was able to speak coolly, as if renowned classicists called me all the time.

An hour later, having been given an eleven o'clock appointment ("I know it's short notice," Ms. Kent said, and I responded, without even a grain of truth, that I'd just had a cancellation), I was sitting in a tastefully appointed outer office, admiring the books and prints. If I had cast my lot differently I could have been part of this genteel environment, instead of spending my days in a cramped second floor box with street noise and no air conditioning. Alice Kent, a woman probably in her early fifties, with thick, graying hair, had told me that

Dr. Benson was on a call and would be with me as soon as he finished. Her phone buzzed, and she lifted the receiver and said, "Ms. Prentice is here, Dr. Benson. Certainly—I'll bring her right in."

She got up and stepped to a door to the right of her desk. I followed her, and waited as she tapped on the door and then opened it. A voice said, "Ms. Prentice, do come in. Thank you, Alice."

Dr. Benson was coming across the room to meet me. He was as I remembered him from the one time we'd met—slight and white-haired, wearing dark slacks, a white shirt and tie, and a cable-knit sweater. A blue blazer hung on a clothes pole next to the door. Imagine working in a place where you actually needed sleeves on an 80-degree day.

" I do appreciate your coming here on so little notice, Ms. Prentice. I'm Alec Benson."

Nothing could have induced me to repeat the falsehood about short notice I'd told Alice. I said, "It's an honor, Professor. Doctor. I have your translation of *Works and Days*. I heard you speak on the Oedipus trilogy."

He laughed. "An extensive choice of seating, as I recall. A colleague later told me my lecture was on the same night as a Celtics game. A championship, I believe he said. My own graduate students were nowhere to be seen. What fables I listened to the next day about expiring grandmothers and kitchen fires and helping sisters to move. At night."

A Hesiod man with a self-deprecating sense of humor. Paying case, nothing—whatever this man wanted was his for the asking.

"Let's sit down," he said. "Would you like coffee?"

It would have been a unique experience to be sipping mid-morning coffee with this man, but I was keyed-up enough without a jolt of caffeine. I said, "No, thank you," and followed him to a deep red sofa between two bookcases. He waited for me to sit, then joined me, leaning his head back for a moment before sitting up straight.

"Now," he said. "Where shall I begin…"

I have several standard approaches to helping potential clients explain why they've called me. This time, I chose the one that was of particular interest to me.

"Where did you hear about my profession, Doctor Benson?"

"From you," he said. I must have looked as surprised as I felt, because he went on, "At the lecture you attended. You asked such an excellent question about Greek burial customs that I thought we must be in the same field. Then when you came up to me afterwards and I asked

25

what college you were affiliated with, you told me you were a private investigator. There was no other woman under that listing in the phone book."

It was coming back to me. I'd been so flattered to be taken as an academic colleague that I'd been a bit reluctant to own up to my real profession. But now it seemed that—*mirabile dictu*—telling the truth had paid off. I said, "And you need a private investigator?"

"I do. The college does." He got up and went to his desk, returning with a folder which he handed to me. Inside was an eight by ten color photograph of an illuminated manuscript.

"Lucretius," I said, my breath catching at the exquisite presentation of the invocation to Venus that opens *De Rerum Natura*.

Mother of the race of Aeneas, delight of men and gods...

"Isn't it beautiful? This is a copy, from the original in the Vatican, of Machiavelli's own manuscript of *De Rerum Natura*, signed by him."

"Are you telling me the college owns"—I indicated the photograph—"this?"

He looked at the photograph, then at me. His eyes, magnified by steel-rimmed glasses, were somber.

"It's disappeared," he said.

CHAPTER EIGHT

"How old is this copy?" I asked.

Dr. Benson's grave expression turned back into a slight smile. "Not five centuries old like the one in the Vatican, but close to half that. A scholar in the late 1700s was given access to Machiavelli's manuscript and granted permission to make a copy. He used parchment and some very delicate inks for authenticity. The copy is quite fragile."

Horace was celebrating the power and immortality of poetry when he described his own work as "a monument more lasting than bronze"—impervious to rain and the north wind and to time itself. But the poetry was the message—very different from the medium that carries the message. It would not take a very prolonged exposure to twenty-first century pollution for this treasure to begin disintegrating.

I said, "Is it possible someone took the manuscript as a prank?"

"Always a possibility with students, especially at this restive end-of-semester time. The young people are stressed with exams and grades, and job hunting for the ones graduating—it's small wonder they do crazy things, often without regard to consequences."

"Do you think a student might have taken the manuscript from… wherever it was kept?"

"Actually," Dr. Benson said, "I don't. Student pranks tend to be highly visible. What fun is it if your friends can't see how you brought a goat into the chapel, or fashioned an elaborate scarecrow of the Dean? Also, the manuscript wouldn't be easily got at. It has to be kept out of sunlight and suitably cool and dry, so we have it in a special locked case, and that room it's in"—he gestured to a door I had assumed led to a closet—"is also kept securely locked. I have the key, and make a point of checking on the rare books in there periodically, and bringing out the Lucretius when it goes on display."

"And how often is that?"

"Once a year. During graduation, when the award given in its donor's name is presented."

The implication of what he had just said was obvious. I asked, "And when is graduation this year?"

"June fifth."

Just over a month away. I asked, "Does the donor attend the award ceremony?"

"His widow does. Mr. Greenberg died two years ago. He was an interesting man—self-made, with that kind of respect for formal education some people have who didn't get much of it themselves. His granddaughters attended Hathorne before it became co-educational, and Mr. Greenberg told our President he appreciated their receiving an education that would allow them to compete in—he used the phrase 'a man's world.' "

Dr. Benson glanced at the photo I was still holding. "The Lucretius was in honor of one granddaughter's majoring in Classics. Mr. Greenberg had a wealthy man's resources, both to locate this manuscript and to place the winning bid when it was auctioned. In addition, he presented the school with a most generous endowment. The exact terms of the gift are confidential, but suffice it to say that because of it, my department is able to concentrate less on constant fund-raising and more on providing the best education to our students."

I asked, "Are there any strings on the endowment?"

Alec Benson smiled at me. "You do get right to the point. In terms of specific conditions or restrictions, no. However, under the terms of Mr. Greenberg's will, his widow has control over the continuation of the endowment."

I was putting this together as best I could and had just been commended for my directness, so I said, "Where do I come in?" Dr. Benson smiled again, approvingly, I thought.

"Where, indeed? As you may have concluded by now, I am most desirous of having the Lucretius back where it belongs in time for the award ceremony at which Mrs. Greenberg will preside. I am also desirous that no one know it was ever missing."

"And you believe no one knows that now? Except for the person who took it?"

28

"I do. My secretary and I have keys to this office, as does the head of Maintenance, and I have two keys to the rare book room"—he again indicated the closed door to the right of his desk. "I carry one key with me, and keep the other at home."

"So," I said. "An inside job."

"It would seem so. To what purpose I have no idea. But the truth of the matter is that Mrs. Greenberg can be quite strong-minded in her role as guardian of her husband's gifts and legacy. I can't imagine that she would be at all pleased to learn we've managed to misplace the irreplaceable."

"So," I said, "You need me to find out as quickly as I can who took the manuscript, and get it back without anyone knowing it was gone."

"Exactly. I realize that last part is the trickiest. You will, after all, at a minimum need to interview the department staff. And this is academia—each person you talk to will talk to a half dozen others, all of them vying to invent and spread the wildest rumors. Since no one can know the real reason you're here we'll have to give them a false reason."

Now he was talking my language. Althea the goddess of truth has never been my patroness, and I warmed to the idea of duplicity. I said, "And do you have one—a false reason?"

"I gave it some thought before contacting you. Why don't I run it by you and you can point out any apparent weaknesses or discrepancies. I'll put the photograph back and get my notes."

I looked one more time at the image of the beautiful missing treasure before closing the folder and handing it to him. He returned it to his desk and came back with a lined page covered with small, calligraphic handwriting.

"The most obvious thing would seem to be the budget," he said. "Alice does an admirable job of managing the accounts and reports, but I was thinking that if someone in the department was able to…hack in… with the intent of misusing funds…"

For once I wasn't the person with the most dismal knowledge of cyberspace. I said, "Professor Benson, it's possible. But it's just as likely someone in Indonesia would have the capability to break into your system."

"Oh." He looked dejected, then smiled again. "Just as I'd hoped— you're already earning your fee by pointing out where the walls of my edifice would crumble. Can you continue on that path by suggesting a more credible cover story?"

Paid to prevaricate—I liked this. "It would have to be something that's physically on the premises," I said. "Not money—I can't imagine you keep much of that lying around—but some sensitive material that would be an embarrassment if its loss were made public."

"The student records," Professor Benson said. I looked at him. "In Alice's files are the paper records of all our current students. Once a student graduates, the records go to a central archives, but until that time we have the only complete set of applications and transcripts for the Classics majors."

"I can see why the loss of that kind of information would be a nuisance, but would it really be cause to call in a private investigator?"

He mulled over my question. Then his face brightened. "Alice."

"Sir?" I said. I'd better begin doing better than this at grasping connections if I wanted to hold on to this new assignment.

"Alice, my secretary. She's well-liked—I'm sure the faculty and graduate students would want to protect her. With everybody so worried these days about identity theft, I could say that if the college administration found out all that personal information was missing, Alice could lose her job."

"Not bad," I said. "There might be some people who wouldn't buy it, but the important thing is that we'd be diverting attention away from what's really missing. You'd tell people you called me because we met at your lecture?"

He nodded. "You promised discretion in looking into this. It's a bonus that you're a classicist yourself."

"Not in the way you and your colleagues are, Professor Benson. I know bits and pieces of the classics—your people are experts."

"Even better," he said. "You'll be able to put my colleagues at ease by asking intelligent questions about their specialties. The one drawback I foresee is that some of them may be so enthusiastic about expounding on their areas of expertise that your eyes will begin glazing over."

"It could work," I said. "And I suppose my not being an ivory tower academic also means that I see the more mundane pitfalls."

"What do you mean?"

I pointed to the closed door that led to the outer office. "Before I begin grilling people about missing files, you need to box up those files and take them home."

CHAPTER NINE

Professor Benson looked startled at what I had said, then pleased. "You are clever," he said. "Imagine if I'd been going on about the files that were missing and somebody just walked over and opened the drawer where they're kept?"

"It's easy not to think of such things when your business isn't subterfuge. But mine is. I can use my experience to keep my clients from tripping themselves up with the kind of details honest, trusting people wouldn't think of."

"You'll do it, then?" Dr. Benson asked. "You'll find out who took the Lucretius and get it back?"

"It will be my golden fleece."

"Splendid." He beamed at me, the very antithesis of a scholar jealously guarding his fiefdom from amateurs. "Let's hope that in your quest for the fleece you encounter far fewer perils than Jason. Of course, part of his reward was being able to display the prize once he'd found it. If all goes as I hope, only you and I will know the manuscript was ever missing."

In my altered state of bantering with a cerebral classicist, I had lost sight of that fact. For a moment, I felt crushed. Never to be surrounded by admiring partygoers eager to hear how Dr. Alec Benson and I had rescued Lucretius. Never to be able to casually display a reference on Hathorne letterhead stating that I was your woman if you were missing a crinkly old parchment.

"About your fee," Dr. Benson said, and my disappointment vanished. Never mind that I'd be toiling in eternal anonymity—I'd take fortune over fame any day. He continued, "I'll be paying you myself. Your fee can hardly come from any college money, and in addition I do feel responsible that the book is missing. And in case you're wondering how I can afford to do this on a professor's salary, I'm very fortunate that circumstances allow me to do what I love without financial concerns."

"Well, that's good," I said, curious, naturally, about the source of such enviable financial freedom. He smiled at me.

"My father invented freeze-dried coffee."

One further thought came to me as I got up to leave and Dr. Benson stood also. "Your secretary. She'll need to know the real story."

"This is going to work," Dr. Benson said approvingly. "You think of all the...angles." He thought for a moment. "I'll take Alice into my confidence. She's been with me for over twenty years and is extremely loyal, both to me and to the department. She will share completely my desire not to have the college embarrassed or the endowment compromised."

I was still going to have to eliminate Alice as a suspect, but this was not the time to get into my detecting methods. Dr. Benson said, "And there is one other thing."

"What's that?" I asked.

"She is far too discreet and professional to ever say so, or show it, but Alice has absolutely no use for Mr. Greenberg's widow."

CHAPTER TEN

I t was noon when I walked out of the Classics department and into the humid day. Before leaving my office to meet with Alec Benson I'd put on my blazer, but now I took it off to carry over my arm. The people crowding the sidewalk in front of the college entrance, many of them not much older than my nephew, looked comfortable in their shorts and T-shirts, and I thought without enthusiasm of my stuffy office. To postpone going back there I looked around for someplace to have lunch.

There were plenty of choices, all of which, in this area of several colleges, looked enticing. A card in the window of one closet-sized place gave the day's special as a fried bologna sandwich with macaroni salad. A Homeric feast by my abysmal standards. But it was crowded, and I hurried past knowing that I'd feel I'd cheated on Tom if I engaged in such an artery-clogging meal.

A block down, there was a wagon with a city permit displayed on its door, and only a short line waiting to sample the vendor's wares. Frozen yogurt—now this was more like it. I got in line behind two girls in denim skirts and halters and read the flavors as the line moved forward. A double chocolate cone sounded like a fine choice, but when my turn came I ordered peach instead, in the largest size, since it was fruit.

I ate my lunch as I walked back to my office, depositing the sticky napkins in the last trash can before my building. As I climbed the stairs with my door key ready in my hand I prepared myself for the blast of hot air awaiting me. But when I opened the door, the air that wafted out was as deliciously cool as if it were blowing straight from snow-covered Olympus.

For a moment, I was too surprised to do anything but stand there with my hand on the doorknob, letting out the chilled air. The landlord's cousin had actually come. When karma decided it was your day, she really did it up right. Quickly, I stepped inside, set my briefcase on the coffee table, and hung up my blazer. Then I sat in my desk chair until even the hair on my head was cool before reaching for the phone.

I got Terry Burke's voice mail—she was probably at lunch—and left a message asking her to call me. When she returned my call at two o'clock she sounded more like her old self—I hoped the change might be due to her knowing she was no longer in this alone. I said, "Terry, did you talk to Russ? About my getting together with him..."

"Last night. You can probably guess that he wasn't too keen on the whole idea. He said..." Terry broke off what she'd been about to say.

"He said it was none of my business," I finished for her. "Precisely the point—if it's none of my business, I do it. If that philosophy were a little shorter I'd have it on my business cards."

Terry laughed. Definitely more like the extroverted lady I knew. I'd have her bingeing on M&M's, her notion of the food of the gods, again in no time. I said, "But he did agree to see me?"

"It was like dealing with Matthew when he's dug in his heels, but yes, he did. Russ is smart enough to know this situation isn't good for any of us. He's stressed out thinking of what's happening with the guys assigned to him, and that has an effect on the kids and me."

"What time do the kids leave for school?" I asked.

"The bus comes for Emmy and Annabelle at 8:15. As soon as they're picked up, Russ drives Matthew to kindergarten."

"So he's back by nine?" I asked. Terry said that he was. "OK," I decided. "Tell him nine o'clock tomorrow morning, please." I didn't want to give Russ any chance to call and put off our meeting. "I'll be at your house then, and we'll start getting to the bottom of this."

34

CHAPTER ELEVEN

On my forty-third birthday I woke to a chilly apartment. In Boston, landlords are allowed to stop providing heat once the probability of raging blizzards has passed—in past unseasonably cold Springs I had suspected my own landlord of lurking next to the furnace at midnight on the appointed day, ready to cut off the heat at the earliest possible second. To think that yesterday I was doing battle with the owner of my office building for air conditioning. The New England climate is not for sissies.

I got up and went into the kitchen, where the coffeemaker was gurgling. Woody greeted me as if I'd been away for years, following my every move as I got his dish out of the dishwasher, filled it with Savory Country Chicken, and set it on the floor. While he purred and ate his breakfast I sat at the counter with my coffee, not taking it back to bed with me since I was meeting with Russ Burke at nine. I quickly moved the cup back when Woody jumped up on the stool next to me, eager to be petted.

"It's my birthday," I told him. "In a few minutes I'm going to check the refrigerator to see what I can have for breakfast. The only criterion is that it not be healthy."

Woody looked as if he was in agreement with this standard, but then, there's very little he doesn't agree with. I went to shower, and found him waiting by the refrigerator when I came back into the kitchen, as if he had understood perfectly what I'd said. Together, we surveyed the birthday breakfast possibilities. Eggs, cheese, milk, some leftover soup. Ketchup and mustard and mayonnaise—nothing to start my heart fluttering. The freezer yielded a far superior option—an unopened pint of Chocolate Fudge Brownie ice cream, along with the cat ice cream I indulgently stock for Woody. I took out both, and opened a drawer for a bowl and spoon.

"I know you want the kind I'm having," I told Woody as he watched my every move, "but chocolate isn't good for cats. For people having a birthday, though, it's a hallowed tradition."

I peeled back the foil from the dish of cat ice cream and set it on the floor. Then I scooped out a hearty serving of my own breakfast, returned the container to the freezer, and settled myself back at the counter, spoon in hand.

"This," I said to my cat, who had finished his own treat and now sat washing his face, "is living."

By quarter of nine I was parked on the street near Russ and Terry's house. A few minutes later I saw their red mini-van coming along the street, its directional blinking for the turn into the Burkes' driveway. Russ saw me and waved, with resignation, I thought, and got out of the van to wait for me on the walk. Once we were inside, he said he needed to move the laundry into the dryer, and asked if I wanted coffee.

"I really need a cup after I've gotten everybody off to school," he said. "Every morning it's such a circus—backpacks, homework, lunches, permission slips. Matthew saying his stomach hurts, Emmy wanting to wear some outfit that shows her midriff." He gave me a rueful smile. "It's only nine o'clock in the morning, and I feel as if I've worked a full day."

I thought of my own peaceful morning routine—a mug of coffee in bed, a book I could read right to the end of a chapter, Woody's company. Of course, that serene start to the day would probably change once Luke started driving, or if Tom and I...

I reminded myself that I was here to work—to do a job for a friend who needed me. Luke and Tom would have to wait their turn. I said to Russ, "Thank you. Coffee would be wonderful."

We sat at the kitchen table, cleared of breakfast dishes but with two boxes of cereal still out. Knowing Terry as I did, it wouldn't have surprised me to find that she ate the cereal with marshmallows and candy in it, while insisting her kids have the nutritious granola with its rainforest-themed box. But who was I, who had brushed her teeth

36

twice to remove all traces of chocolate, to be critiquing other people's food choices?

"This is good coffee," I said to Russ. "You must have known your way around the kitchen even before you left your job."

I was deliberately getting straight to the point, but Russ, who was well aware of what I'd come to talk about, chose to respond to my bit of small talk about the coffee.

"My schedule's always been more flexible than Terry's," he said. "We both pitched in in the morning getting the kids up and fed and to school with everything they were supposed to have. Actually, Terry had the one job you couldn't pay me to do—getting Emmy out of bed. That's one grumpy kid in the morning, even before she shut down emotionally when Oliver..." He broke off, then said, "Anyway, I had the easy part—making the coffee and getting the other two kids to the table."

"Tell me about Oliver, Russ," I said. "I don't mean how he died—Terry told me that. It must have been awful for all of you—but why would you think you were responsible?"

Instead of answering, he got up and went to the counter, coming back with the coffeepot. I nodded and thanked him when he held the pot over my cup, then waited while he poured more coffee for himself and carried the empty pot to the sink.

"It's the kind of thing we have training for," he said, when he was back at the table, holding his coffee cup but not drinking from it. "Boundaries. Limits. Keeping a professional distance so you don't become your patient's pal." He looked at me, his expression one of pain. "I didn't keep to any of those things with Oliver. I brought him home with me, and Terry and the kids loved him, so I encouraged him to visit here all the time. He and Terry were always laughing about something, and the way he could draw Emmy out without even trying..."

Russ drew in a breath and let it out. "I made him into my little brother instead of my patient. We even talked about making a day of it taking Matthew to his first Red Sox game. It was all so normal that I lost sight of how fragile he was, after what he'd been through. How could he have thought he could talk to me as his therapist when I'd made him into my kids' favorite uncle?"

I waited to be certain he wasn't going to say anything more, then I said, "What do you mean, Russ, by 'after what he'd been through'? I've seen the images on television, but I don't think anyone who hasn't served in a war zone can begin to imagine what that's like. Was there some specific incident that left him…fragile?"

"No," Russ said, so quickly that I raised my eyebrows at him.

"You don't have to stop to think about it? Go back over your sessions with him?"

"Look," he said, "I told you. This was my fault. If I'd kept my professional distance with Oliver he might still be alive. He had such empathy for other people—he'd never have wanted to upset a friend by talking about it when the bottom started falling out of his life." Russ looked angry, almost certainly at himself. "After all, that's what therapists are for."

"Even if you're right," I said, "and my opinion is that you're blaming yourself far too much, you've been doing this work for years. You've helped your patients put their lives back together, and then when one of them…"

"When one of them needs me and can't come to me," Russ interrupted, which was not what I'd been going to say. "Well, that one was Oliver. I let him down and now he's dead and it's not going to happen again."

It was time to stop for today. I could have gone on by suggesting there may have been things going on in Oliver's life that he wouldn't even disclose to a counselor, but Russ wasn't ready to listen, much less to forgive himself. I got up from the table.

"Let's leave this for now," I said. "But, Russ, I want to come again. Terry's worried about you, and she's worried about the kids. If I could talk to the kids, at least I might be able to get a sense of how all this is affecting them."

"What are you going to tell Terry?" Russ asked, reaching for my coffee cup to take to the sink with his own.

"That we talked," I said. "That I can see you love her and the kids and want everybody to get past this. That I'm going to come back here…" and before he could react to that, "…and that, to use one of my favorite aphorisms…Rome wasn't built in a day."

CHAPTER TWELVE

drove home—positively no other business appointments on my birthday—and made a cup of tea to sip while I mulled over my Hathorne assignment. I needed to focus on how to interview people without their becoming defensive—maybe I could start by asking the faculty members how they chose a career in Classics. I jotted a note on the lined pad I was resting on Woody's back. For my birthday dinner Tom was taking me to a heavenly Italian restaurant, after which we were going back to his place. I was looking forward to both events, but for now, I loved the solitude of having my own private space with just Woody as a live-in.

"It could work," I told my cat, in his function of consultant as well as writing table. "Start with how everybody got into Classics, on to how they all ended up at Hathorne, and finally, I hope, end with a few disclosures about who, if anyone, has it in for Professor Benson and might not mind using his secretary as a scapegoat."

Before I could go much further with my idea I needed to run it by Professor Benson, who knew best the people I would be talking to, so I lifted my pad and nudged Woody off my lap, put what I had written in my desk, and went to make some lunch. My apartment had warmed up a little since I had awakened in the cold, but the chicken noodle soup I heated in the microwave still tasted good. I was just finishing it when the phone rang—Martha, calling to wish me a happy birthday and to find out whether Luke's present for me had arrived.

"I haven't checked the mail yet," I said. "There'll be a slip if the super has something for me. But tell me about you. What do you have on for today? How's Iris, my discerning new cat friend?"

Iris, Martha said, was fine and was at the moment in the kitchen window watching the birdfeeder with great intensity while the birds, perhaps with generations of learned knowledge of the purpose of a window, were ignoring her. Martha herself was picking up two friends for a lunch at McDonald's.

"Not my first choice," Martha said, "but it's nice that Trudy and Eleanor want to get out. They're both in their eighties now and are getting a little fond of staying home all the time."

Martha herself would be eighty-three in a month, and life just seemed to get more interesting for her every year. I said, "I'm completely loyal to Burger King. I'll let you be off, and go see if that package came. Tom said you helped with it, so thank you."

"That nephew of yours is a wonderful boy," Martha said. "I just came up with the general plan, and he did the rest."

And you made sure he had enough money for it, I thought but didn't say. When friends come bearing gifts and then want someone other than themselves to get the credit, I try to treat such gestures as added gifts.

"Enjoy your day," I said to Martha. "I love you."

"I love you, too, Nell. Have a good time tonight."

When I went downstairs to my mailbox the slip for a package was there, along with some bills and two pastel envelopes that must be birthday cards. I headed to the basement and claimed a box that was large but not heavy, addressed to me in Luke's awkward handwriting that resembled his father's. Back upstairs I put the box on the kitchen table, where Woody eyed it as I went to get a knife.

"The box is your present," I told him. "Just as soon as I see what's in it."

Luke had sent me a dark blue nylon jacket with the name and logo of his school on the breast pocket. Holding it up, seeing that Martha must have told him the correct size, I felt a sense of connection with my small family. I had a kid at this school, and when I wore the jacket and people asked about it I could tell them about Luke and how he and I had found each other. I went to the phone and dialed a number I knew by heart. Luke must have been in class—that was the only time he was ever parted from his phone—so I left a voice mail message.

"Luke? It's Aunt Nell. I absolutely love the jacket. It's the perfect birthday present—thank you so much. I wish you were here, but you will be soon, and we'll drive to Maine and you can tell me everything that's going on…"

Oh, God, I imagined him thinking, listening to me blithely assume he was going to tell me anything, much less everything, about his sixteen-year-old life. I fumbled to a graceless close before I could render myself even more clueless. "Anyway, thanks again. I love you."

I put the phone down. Clueless I might be, but I did love Luke and Martha and Tom. I was forty- three years old, exactly, and had in my life a woman and a man and a boy who had moved me past grief and loss to where I was now.

"And you," I called to my cat, who was scratching the inside of the box so that a few cardboard flakes flew out. "I love the world's best cat."

Tom picked me up at six. He was wearing a summer suit and a tie that, unplanned, was a few shades deeper than my pale green dress. He smiled when he saw my overnight bag next to the door.

"So I get to have you for the whole rest of your birthday," Tom said, holding out a hand to Woody, who quickly abandoned his cardboard box. "Is this fellow all set? Maybe we should bring him to my place…"

"Tom," I said, "Woody will be fine. He's had ice cream, and his food and water are fresh, and his heated pillow is working. He has new toys. I'll come back here early tomorrow so you and I can both get to work, but for tonight—just the two of us, please."

Tom gave Woody a final pat and came to put his arms around me. We stood like that for a minute or two, then I kissed him and said, "Before we go—wait until you see what Luke sent me."

CHAPTER THIRTEEN

Paisano's, on the south shore of Boston, is my favorite restaurant. Delicious food, a charming ambience, and a Greek owner with whom I had once discussed the pronunciation differences between ancient and modern Greek. When we had ordered—I barely glanced at the menu before settling on the Fettuccini Neptune—I took Tom's hand and said, "I love coming here. It always makes me want to go to Rome. To see all that civilization I've read about, try the food…"

"They have cats, too," Tom said. "Everywhere, from what I've heard. You could bring back a sultry Italian girlfriend for Woody."

Not long ago I might have joked that Woody could fend for himself—what about a handsome *signore* for me? But I didn't want a sexy foreign lover who would sweep me off my feet. I wanted what I had—Tom.

"We should really do it," I said. "Take a trip together. Go somewhere neither of us has ever been."

"We wouldn't need to hire a guide," Tom said. "I'd have my own classicist to show me around Italy."

"And you could bond with the *carabinieri*," I said. "Compare notes on how law enforcement is done in Massachusetts and in a country whose traditions go so far back. We'd have a good time." I smiled at him, and squeezed the hand I was holding. "We're good together."

"We are," Tom agreed, as our wine appeared in a bucket. We let the waiter go through his ceremony of getting our approval of the wine before filling our glasses, which we raised to each other as soon as the waiter left.

"To you, Nell," Tom said. "Happy birthday."

"To us," I responded. "The happy part."

The meal, from appetizers through entrees to lemon ice box cake, was one to linger over. Tom and I talked easily, enjoying the exquisite food and each other's company. When we finally left the restaurant there was a fog blowing past as we walked hand in hand to Tom's car.

"I had it washed," Tom said as he opened the passenger door for me. "But maybe what I really should have done was spring for one of those stretch limos."

"Those are for the prom," I said, smoothing my dress as I got into the car and Tom went around to the driver's side. "Which I didn't go to, and which, I point out, I am a quarter century too old for. But I have no regrets." I smiled at him as he fastened his seat belt. "You are my ideal in a guy, and your Ford Bronco is all a woman could want in a chariot."

Back at his place, I agreed to a nightcap, and was touched to see Tom bring out an unopened bottle of expensive-looking brandy, with snifters. As we sat on the sofa sipping our drinks I leaned my head back in contentment and said, "A perfect day."

"Good. That's what I wanted you to have. God knows we both have enough work days that are anything but perfect."

When he said that, I thought of the work day I'd had only twenty-four hours earlier. "Tom," I said. "About work—I've picked up a case that's pretty unusual." I could tell he was listening intently, and to lighten the mood I said, "I'm getting paid for it—that can be unusual in itself…" I was stalling, and when Tom didn't say anything in response to my levity I drew in a breath and got ready to tell him what I meant by 'unusual.'

"Here's the thing. Of course you and I don't talk about our active cases, except for anything that's already public. But with this case, if I'm successful, I'll never be able to talk about it. Unless I screw up, that is—in that case you'll be able to read about it in the papers along with everybody else."

"Then I guess I won't be hearing about it," Tom said. I looked at him gratefully, appreciating his expression of confidence in me and the way it didn't occur to him to press me for more information than I was comfortable giving. I went on, "It's also a very time-sensitive case. In just a few weeks I'll be able to tell you if it's all worked out and I'm in a position to buy you a gourmet dinner with my fee."

"Sounds good," Tom said, and yawned. "Sorry. It really does sound interesting." I laughed, and found myself yawning from contagion. I put down my brandy snifter and stood, holding out my hand.

"Enough of mysterious cases. Let us be off to bed. I call to your attention that I am forty-three years old—a creakingly advanced age in classical times. Virgil was only…"

Tom stood and put his arms around me and his mouth on mine. All thought of my age, and of Virgil, vanished.

CHAPTER FOURTEEN

om wanted to drive me home, but I told him there was no need—the subway, safe enough at rush hour, would take me to within a few blocks of my door. I put on jeans and a T-shirt, folded my dress carefully into my overnight bag, and gave Tom a long kiss goodbye.

"Have a good day," I said. "I'll call you tonight. And thank you."

"My pleasure," he said. "Let's hope Woody's not too mad at me for monopolizing you."

Woody was, of course, no such thing. He met me at the door with his tail held high and bumped his head against my leg, purring, as soon as I was inside. I scooped him up and let him nuzzle my face.

"You good boy," I said. " I had a wonderful birthday, but now I'm glad to be home and to see you and have you keep me company while I have breakfast."

I hadn't been exaggerating when I told Tom that time was of the essence in finding answers in my new case. Graduation at Hathorne was exactly a month away, which probably accounted for Professor Benson's sounding so pleased to hear from me when I called him as soon as I got home. We agreed I would come by his office at one.

"I have faculty evaluations to conduct all morning—the Sisyphean curse of being a department head," he explained. I would present my approach, and if it sounded good to Professor Benson, I could begin interviewing members of his department on Friday.

"There are still exams and meetings with students," he went on, "But the faculty will be dispersing very soon, especially those who will be away, or are traveling between the end of classes and graduation."

After my phone call I showered, then had my oatmeal and coffee in my armchair so that Woody, deprived of my company for an entire night, could sit in my lap. In mid-morning, when it was late enough that I wouldn't hit subway rush hour a second time in one day, I took the train into my office and did some paperwork before leaving at 12:30 for my appointment at Hathorne. I picked up a bagel on the way to the subway stop, not wanting to be tempted by the fried bologna special in the student neighborhood I was headed into. You'd think that after a divine meal at Paisano's the night before I would think with revulsion of fried bologna, but in matters of gourmandism, there's not much hope for me.

In the Classics office Alice Kent beamed at me as I came through the door. "Ms…" she began, then stopped speaking as if this were just all too exciting for words. I managed not to laugh—in my line of work I'm used to subterfuge, but it must be a nice change for a Classics Department secretary to be transformed from keeper of calendar and phone messages into Mata Hari. I smiled in return to let her know that yes, it was just the three of us who knew the real story.

"And here is our *adiutrix*." It was Professor Benson's voice—Alice and I both turned to see him standing in the doorway of his office. "I now understand fully why the Romans made that word feminine. Suffice it to say that here is our helper."

His including Alice in our little band of Latinists was not lost on her—if she got any more enthusiastic she was going to need smelling salts. No doubt noticing this, Professor Benson said to me, "Let's just go into my office, then." To Alice he added, "And just as soon as we've settled on the details we'll be wanting to bring you in on them."

We left Alice as sparkling-eyed as any *glaukopis* Athena and went into Professor Benson's office. I asked him how his faculty evaluations had gone.

"Well enough," he said. "It's the part of my job I like least. So much jockeying for position, with tenure as the prize." He smiled at me. "A different kind of golden fleece."

As I began sharing my further thoughts on the ruse behind which I would conduct my interviews, I resolved to be alert to any suggestion that a faculty member had not been fairly treated in the performance review process. As I outlined what I had come up with, I was pleased to see my listener nodding in apparent approval.

46

"As you pointed out," I began, "an internal investigation like this one usually involves financial improprieties. A person—authorized or not—having access to funds and transferring them into a personal account, all while ingeniously covering up the trail of electronic bread crumbs. Or internet porn, 900 numbers—that sort of thing."

Professor Benson laughed. "We have several MENSA members on faculty, but their academic brilliance doesn't necessarily mean they can balance their own checkbooks, much less perform financial skullduggery online. As to pornography, as a Classics department we have been known to encounter a unique problem. A professor will want to download a classical image for use in class, and the software filtering system—archaic in the very worst sense—will block access simply because the human figure is nude."

"I've seen some of those figures in the MFA," I said. "They don't set off the alarms, but people stand there with their mouths open, then hustle the kids back to the mummies. In any case, what we've come up with seems to be our best decoy—a story of missing student files, the possibility of identity theft, that could get Alice, and you as her supervisor, into trouble. As I talk to people I'll listen for any sign that the person I'm talking to may be harboring hostility toward you. The ones who are happy here would want this situation resolved quickly and quietly, without embarrassment to the department. Should I let people know you're footing the bill yourself?"

He thought about that. "That might be best. It wouldn't do if a staff member already unhappy about the size of his or her raise were to think I was blowing the salaries budget on a detective."

"And Alice can provide me with the information on who got the smaller raises and who is still waiting for a promotion?"

"I'll be sure she knows I want her to give you all the help she can. She's efficient and discreet. I'll have her get together the faculty schedules and departure dates so you can begin your interviews right away."

"Begin when the time is ripe for your undertaking," I said.

Professor Benson looked momentarily startled, then delighted. "My own translation!" he said. "Oh, I certainly wish the manuscript had never disappeared in the first place, but what an adventure having you appear as our Achilles to save the day."

"I'm glad you think of me as Achilles rather than Hector," I said. "Although neither one of them exactly lived to see old age." What would the feminine versions of those names be, I wondered. Achillea? Hectress?

"But both are remembered as heroes," Professor Benson said. "Now let us take advantage of the ripeness—and the shortness—of time. This afternoon I shall call together all members of the department and have them give Alice their availability to be interviewed."

He smiled at me. "And speaking of Alice, I believe we are ready to bring her in to learn her part in all this." He leaned forward in his desk chair and touched a phone button.

"Alice? Could you please join us in my office? No, no note pad. What we will be discussing is in strictest confidence."

CHAPTER FIFTEEN

left the Hathorne Classics Department with two things—a check drawn on Professor Benson's personal account, and a college catalog. Two of the faculty and one assistant taught classes on Friday, and Alice was going to arrange for me to meet with them after their classes. I deposited the check before taking the subway back to my office, where I brewed a pot of coffee and settled in to read about the people I would be interviewing the next day.

Milo Franklin was a full professor of Ancient History who had been with Hathorne seventeen years. There was a photo of him in a book-lined study—he looked to be in his fifties, bald and clean-shaven. Beneath the photo was an impressive listing of its subject's credentials, books, and articles. Next was Sarah Wingate. She had been with Hathorne five years—a serious-looking African-American woman who, the entry said, taught a course in Latin poets and one in Women in Antiquity. She was an assistant professor, with a brief list of articles to her credit. The teaching assistant was named Gabe Chan, probably a Chinese surname. There was no photo or additional information on him in the catalog, so I would need to wait until tomorrow to find out whether my assumption was correct. I put the catalog in my briefcase and took several folders I had been working on out of my desk drawer, firmly shifting my concentration away from the appealing prospect that I would be meeting at least three more classicists the next day.

I worked until after six, and called Tom just before leaving my office. He was likely to still be in his office, but Naomi, the department secretary who always sounded curious about Tom's and my relationship, would have gone home. Sometimes I thought I was just as curious myself about that subject.

"Hi, Nell," Tom said when he answered his direct line. "As you seem to have guessed, I'm still here. Crime is pretty light here in the suburbs compared to Boston, but what there is comes with plenty of triplicate paperwork. Are you home?"

"Just leaving my office," I said. "I have my own paperwork for tonight, so I wanted to call you before I got too immersed in it. What about dinner at my place on Saturday?"

"Sounds good. Want to go to a movie first?"

Saturday was predicted to be sunny and warm. Tom was supposed to be getting regular exercise, and it certainly wouldn't hurt me to begin working off the calories from last night's extravagant meal. I said, "Why don't we meet in the city around noon? We could take a walk in the Garden and the Common, then come back to my place."

"Okay," Tom agreed. "It's never a bad idea to have a cop with you when you're spending time on the Common."

"It's fine during the day," I said, springing like Hector to the defense of my city. "It will be all joggers and bicyclists and people like us."

"What's the 'like us' part?"

"People who like being together," I said, and went quickly on to where we might meet, before Tom could offer any commentary about what 'being together' actually meant.

Woody approved completely of my evening research project. Instead of a book, dictionary, pad, and pen, I had only a small, neat catalog to read while my cat sat comfortably in my lap. His eyes were closed, but I was sure he was listening attentively to my running commentary.

"Milo Franklin," I told Woody, "seems to have it all. He's full professor with plenty of seniority, not to mention tenure and a full list of publications. But is he discontented in any way? Did he think he would be head of the department by now? And then—" I turned the page—"there's Sarah Wingate. An African-American woman. An affirmative action hire? Any subtle or not so subtle discrimination going on that she thinks Professor Benson should be doing more to discourage?"

Woody opened his eyes and made a sound like a squeak toy.

"You're right," I told him. "All idle speculation. I need to put aside any and all preconceptions and approach Milo Franklin, Sarah Wingate, and Gabriel Chan with my unfailingly professional open mind and see what I can trick out of them."

CHAPTER SIXTEEN

"Ms. Prentice, this is Gabriel Chan. Mr. Chan, Nell Prentice. I've asked Ms. Prentice to help us with the problem I discussed at yesterday's meeting."

It was 10 A.M. on Friday, and I was in a small conference room being introduced by Professor Benson to Gabe Chan, who had just taught the 8 A.M. section of first-year Latin. Gabe Chan was short—no more than five feet five, I estimated—wearing a teaching assistant uniform of button-down shirt, striped tie, chinos, and moccasins. He looked to be in his mid-twenties, of Asian descent, and his expression was polite but reserved as we shook hands.

"I appreciate your time, Gabe," Professor Benson said. "I've outlined Ms. Prentice's objective to you but she'll be able to fill in the details. Shall I have Alice bring coffee?"

Most graduate students I've known would never pass on free refreshments—I've been to college parties at which you'd think a plague of locusts had descended on the food—but Gabe Chan, turning his polite look on Professor Benson, said, "No, thank you."

"Ms. Prentice?" Professor Benson asked, and I also declined, though I would have welcomed the social element that having coffee with this young man might provide.

"I'll leave you to get started, then." Professor Benson smiled at each of us and went out, closing the door behind him. Gabe Chan, sitting opposite me at the small round table, was clearly going to wait for me to speak first.

"Thank you for agreeing to talk to me, Mr. Chan," I said. "Professor Benson told you about the missing files?"

He nodded. It was a good thing Professor Benson and I had gotten our stories straight. Gabe Chan was certainly polite, but I doubted anyone would ever describe him as forthcoming.

"Do you have any thoughts on who might have removed the files from Professor Benson's office?"

He shook his head. I felt encouraged by the fact that he seemed to accept that the files, safe in Dr. Benson's house, were actually missing. I eased into finding out what I could about this young man's attitude toward where he spent his working days. "Most people your age I know are majoring in computers or finance, not classics."

He didn't respond to this implied question. What a witness he would make. I said, "How did you choose a major in classics?"

He answered me, finally, appearing to choose his words carefully.

"I like languages. I was born in California, and my parents and my sister and I spoke English at home, but we also were expected to know Chinese, out of respect for our grandparents." Two entire sentences—a voluble outpouring in contrast to a few minutes ago. "And Latin's so sensible," he said. "So much more comprehensible than an uninflected language like English."

"Man bites dog," I said. Gabe Chan looked startled.

"In English," I said, "with no case endings, word order is crucial. But in Latin *homo mordet canem* means the opposite of *hominem mordet canis*, no matter what order the words are in."

He laughed. "My students will love that one." Rapport at last. Gabe actually began offering information without my even needing to ask questions. He liked Hathorne, liked the faculty, particularly Professor Benson. He felt that the graduate teaching assignments were fairly distributed. He was writing his thesis on the Punic wars and hoped that after getting his degree he would be able to find a teaching position at the college or junior college level.

"It would be funny if I end up somewhere like the Midwest," he told me. "Here, there are plenty of students and a few faculty who look like me, not to mention a whole section of Boston that's almost completely Chinese-American. But I'd probably stand out in a place like Iowa or Kansas."

"But you do feel that you fit in here? That you're part of the Hathorne community?"

53

"Sure," he said. "Everybody's been encouraging about my goals. Professor Benson says he'll write me a good reference when I start looking for jobs. I'm not likely to find one in the Northeast, though—too much competition."

"You'll be following in a great classical tradition," I said. "Off on your odyssey, to see a different world. I wish you lots of adventures, Gabe."

I asked him to stop by the Classics Department office and let Alice know I was ready to talk to Sarah Wingate, whose appointment with me was for ten-thirty, just a few minutes away.

Sarah Wingate was quite formally dressed, in a cranberry suit with a skirt, white blouse and black low heels, and a silver necklace with matching earrings. Professor Benson introduced us, and asked me to stop by his office when Ms. Wingate and I were finished.

I was genuinely interested in the courses Ms. Wingate was teaching, particularly the one on Women in Antiquity, but I decided to save any comment on that subject for later in our talk. I've had women try to bond with me on no basis other than our shared gender and don't particularly care for it. I didn't want to get off on the wrong foot if Sarah Wingate felt the same way. I asked her about the student files and she told me she had no idea where they might be. I then went on to the question that had yielded results with Gabe Chan. I asked, "How did you decide to study Classics?"

"My mother was a high-school Latin teacher. She had me started on vocabularies when I was in the third grade, so by the time I got to high school I had a good head start on Latin and I stayed with it. Of course"—she looked at me as if to assess my reaction to what she was about to say—"I went through a phase of wanting to be anything but what my mother was. But here I am..."

"A college professor," I said, and stopped myself from adding *Your mother must be so proud*. It would have sounded definitely patronizing, as if she'd just told me she'd worked her way up from the cotton fields. Would I have ever made such an observation to a white male?

What Ms. Wingate said next surprised me. "Sometimes I wish I had decided to follow in her footsteps by becoming a high school teacher."

"Why is that?" I asked, when it was evident she wasn't going to explain her remark unless I asked.

"It sounds so clichéd, but my Mom made a difference. She taught in a school with a low graduation rate, but her Latin classes were always small and the kids in them were bright and had the best chance of breaking the cycle—poverty, drugs, dropping out. My mother wasn't just a good teacher—she was the person who listened and encouraged and even brought kids home if there was nowhere else for them to go. Just about all of them graduated, and quite a few went to college.

"Here," Sarah Wingate gestured at the well-appointed conference room, possibly paid for with the endowment I was trying to help Professor Benson preserve, "most of the students have had a pretty smooth life. A home, parents, food and travel and..." she paused, as if to summon just the right word, "security. They've been told every day how special they are, and they look at college as one more thing they're owed. You don't want to know the kind of things they write on their evaluation of my courses."

Oh, but I did. "Negative comments?" I asked.

"You could call it that. I'm too strict about attendance. I don't encourage their creativity. I assign too much homework and expect them to do sight-reading. I don't think some of these kids would be satisfied unless I came in every day and spent fifty minutes telling them how wonderful they are."

I said, "Do the student evaluations count for much when you're evaluated by your department head?"

"With some it would," Sarah Wingate said. "The insidious thing about student complaints is that they can be really useful if your boss doesn't want to give you a raise or a promotion, or even wants to get rid of you. But Doctor Benson isn't anything like that. He actually thinks I'm doing my job when I expect students to act like young adults and do the work in my class if they want a good grade." She smiled at me. "He says if the students weren't complaining about me he'd think I was slipping."

It certainly looked as if I could cross another name off my list of people who might have a grudge against Professor Benson. Now that my interview was at an end and I didn't have to concern myself with sounding like a flatterer I was able to say, "There's one more thing, Professor. The courses you teach sound really interesting. Do you think I could sit in on each of them some time? I'd promise to write you a really first-rate evaluation."

She laughed. "I'd like that. Right now, these last few classes are just for review of course material before exams, but in the Fall you'd be most welcome."

Her response made me realize that, unless my inquiries produced the desired result, I might in the very near future find myself *persona non grata* at the Hathorne Classics Department. I put that thought aside and recalled a saying quoted by Marcus Aurelius. *Get the work in hand done well*. Well and quickly, I emended.

I remembered that Professor Benson had asked me to stop by after meeting with Sarah Wingate, so I walked the short distance from the conference room to his office, where I found Alice at her desk.

"Hi, Alice. Professor Benson wanted to see me."

"Oh," she said. "Ms. Prentice—" She stopped, and gave a nervous giggle.

"Nell, " I said.

"Nell," she repeated. "Actually—Nell—it's not Professor Benson who wanted to ask you something, it's me. Professor Franklin won't be here until two, and unless you had plans or were going back to your office, I wondered if you'd like to go to lunch with me."

This seemed to me an opportunity to be seized upon. I'd get to talk to Alice in a friendly, informal setting, in a lunchtime conversation rather than an interview. And there'd be food.

"I have my car," she was saying. "There's a place a couple of miles from here..."

Even better. Privacy, and not much chance of being overheard by anyone associated with Hathorne.

"It's mostly burgers and subs and that kind of thing," Alice said. "Unless you're a vegetarian...?"

"Alice," I said, "I am as much a vegetarian as the guys in Homer roasting whole oxen in a pit. Lead on."

CHAPTER SEVENTEEN

Alice's car was a red Corolla with a passenger door that stuck. "I should trade this thing in," she told me, reaching across to open the door from the inside. "Oh—wait." She brushed at the passenger seat. "My dog rides up in front when we go places. Look at all this hair…"

I got in, thinking I must remember to brush off my dark blue skirt before meeting Milo Franklin. "I have a cat," I told Alice. "Pet hair makes me feel right at home. What kind of dog is it?"

The restaurant was just what I'd hoped for as a setting for a private conversation. It wasn't crowded, and when I asked the waitress for a booth she showed us to one in a far corner, away from the entryway and the bar. The menu was varied—I skipped past Salads and Lighter Fare and at once spotted my dream choice.

"A meatball sub," I said to Alice. "That's what I'm going to have." It was probably one of the poorest choices I could make, since it put me at risk of arriving for my meeting with Professor Franklin besmirched with Marinara sauce and dog hair. But it came with fries, and I wanted it.

"I guess I'll have the chili dog," Alice said, rendering my own choice practically sophisticated. We ordered, and since Alice had been the one to suggest our having lunch together, I started by asking, "Was there something you wanted to talk to me about?"

"Just the…case," Alice said. She sounded self-conscious using the word, but that's what it was called. "Professor Benson told me that if you can find the Lucretius so it's back before graduation you won't get any credit. You'd get paid, of course. He told me about that—as if I'd ever think for one minute that he'd use the college's money. But he'd be the only one to know." She met my eyes—hers were such a bright blue that I was pretty sure she was wearing contact lenses. "But I'd know, too. I'd know what you did for him."

It was beginning to look like a Herculean task to find anybody who didn't think Professor Benson was the greatest. I said, "You think a lot of him?"

"He gave me a chance when my life was upside down. My husband had just left me for a student. My kids were three and five. I needed a job if I was going to keep a roof over our heads, and I practiced for the interview here until I had my script memorized."

I felt very indignant. What about alimony and child support? Had this cad just been allowed to walk away from his responsibilities with no consequences? But I knew I needed to let Alice tell her story without interruption.

"Professor Benson was making small talk, asking me about my children, and he said he'd enjoyed those preschool years in his own children and I started to pick up where I'd left off and instead of telling him how good a typist I was or whatever was supposed to come next, I started to cry.

"I couldn't believe that was happening. I was positive I'd blown the interview. I started apologizing and pulling tissues out of my purse. I'd never get the job now—who'd want to hire someone who was such an emotional basket case? When Professor Benson got up and went out of his office I was sure he was just going to have somebody else come to tell me that we were through.

"But then he came back in. He had gone to get me a cup of water. When I started again to apologize, he said that we'd just start over. He said he'd gotten nervous himself in plenty of interviews. Can you believe anyone being so nice, Ms—Nell?"

'Nice' barely covered it. A lot of interviewers would count out a candidate just because she had children, never mind one who burst into tears at the interview. I said, "And you've been with the Department for twenty years now?"

"Twenty-two. My girls are all grown up—one works in a bank, and the other's a nurse. I'm about to become a grandmother."

I was still thinking about the dastardly ex. Was there a chance he was somehow mixed up in this, trying to hurt Alice through the job she clearly loved? I said, "And does your ex-husband know he's about to become a grandfather?"

Alice shot me a look of utter scorn. "The guy who never so much as sent his daughters a birthday card? For a while I made sure there was always an extra present 'from Daddy,' but they stopped asking about him, and I stopped pretending. A man has to be a father before he can call himself a grandfather. Anyway, what I'm saying is that none of the good things in my life would have happened if it hadn't been for Professor Benson. If the girls were sick, if my parents needed me as they got older, Professor Benson would tell me to do whatever I needed for my family. He said..." She concentrated, wanting to quote him exactly, "that there's a good piece of advice from the classics. *Someday even this will be a joy to remember.*"

Virgil. I've clung to that phrase myself more than once, as tightly as the Trojans are clinging to the wreckage of their ships when their leader makes his promise. I said, "You and I are after the same thing, Alice. We both want to see this situation resolved so there's no trouble for Professor Benson, now or ever." She nodded vigorously, and I said, "Tell me..."

A delicious aroma came wafting toward us. I stopped talking while the waitress set out our sandwiches and iced tea. When she'd left, Alice and I both pulled a half dozen napkins from the dispenser before starting in on our food.

"Oh, this is good," I said, cutting tiny bites of sub roll with meatballs and melted Parmesan, a nicety required to avoid drips. Fastidious or not, I was finished before Alice was. I sighed contentedly, wiped my mouth and hands with a few more napkins, and went back to what I'd been about to say when the food arrived.

"Alice, you and I are speaking in confidence." She nodded, and a bit of chili sauce dripped onto her placemat. "You've been here long enough so that you must have pretty good impressions of everybody. Can you think of anyone who might want to cause trouble for Professor Benson?" I saw how hesitant she looked and said, "Anything you can tell me doesn't go any further. Not even back to Professor Benson."

She thought about my question for a moment. Then she said, "Everybody likes him. It's not just me he treats like a human being—it's everybody. Of course, he's responsible for performance evaluations, and he won't give a good reference to a student who hasn't earned it. How else could he be?" she asked, as if I'd been about to find fault with this conduct. "He's fair, and he's ethical."

"Any students you can think of who didn't get the reference they were after?"

"Nothing comes to mind," Alice said, after having stopped to think about my question. "Professor Benson really tries to work out any problems, with the faculty and the students, before they get out of hand. If things reached a point where he couldn't write a decent reference, the person would probably already know that and not even ask."

And you, I thought, are his faithful Achates. Captain Aeneas's unwaveringly loyal companion. I was depending on that loyalty to elicit an answer to my next question and what it implied.

"Do people talk to you about their evaluations?"

The look she gave me wasn't just hesitant this time—her expression closed up in such a way I thought she might refuse to answer. I said, "We don't have much time, Alice. It would help a lot if you could give me any idea who might have a grudge against Professor Benson."

She was weighing my comment. Probably she wished she'd stuck with the vending machines instead of asking me to go to lunch with her. She sighed, and said, "I'd never call it a grudge, but Professor Franklin did write a comment on his evaluation—not the one yesterday, but the one before that, from last year. He said that he was the most prolific faculty member when it comes to published articles, and he thought his salary increase should reflect that."

"Did he get his wish this year?"

Alice shook her head. "Even with the endowment, the Department is on a pretty tight budget when it comes to salaries. There'd be too much jealousy from the other departments if our salaries were higher than anybody else's. Professor Franklin must know that."

"Knowing it doesn't mean he has to like it," I said. "He may think Professor Benson could be doing more to get him what he deserves. I'll see if I can lead him into going into that." I held up a hand as I noticed Alice's alarmed expression. "Without, of course, bringing you into it in any way. Anybody else?"

It was pretty clear from her expression that there was somebody else she was thinking of. I said, "Alice? Between the two of us? To help Professor Benson?"

"Libby Morse," she said, after looking around and lowering her voice. "She was at Yale, and there was some kind of falling out and she ended up here. A personality conflict, I heard her telling somebody. I thought she might have forgotten I was there and might overhear, but

60

it's more likely she just didn't care about any opinion I'd have. She acts like she's slumming. And she's always telling people it's an old boys network in the Department even though—" Alice's voice became very firm, "—it's not."

"This is a big help," I said. "And I promise you don't have to worry that your name will come up. In fact..." I glanced around with my best imitation of a mysterious spy— "...we're not even here." I pointed to the white platter that had held my meatball sub—a single mashed French fry was all that remained on the plate. "I am not a person who would ever order this adolescent meal."

Alice laughed. "It's after one—we should head back. After all, we'll have to go in separately—no being seen together."

She wanted to split the cost of lunch with me, but I insisted on paying. It's not very often a person can get reliable information for the cost of a chili dog. As we walked to her car I found myself thinking of the quotation from Virgil, and hoped it would apply in this case, even if there would be only three of us doing the remembering.

Forsan et haec, olim meminisse iuvabit

To paraphrase, for all we know, we'll look back on this and laugh.

CHAPTER EIGHTEEN

lice dropped me off in front of the campus bookstore, where I intended to lurk long enough for her to be comfortably back at her desk when I arrived as if from a solitary lunch. The bookstore contained a beguiling section of Classics, including a textbook for a Mythology course to which Alec Benson had contributed a piece titled *Dionysus: God of Great Cheer.* I considered buying the book and asking Professor Benson to sign it, but rejected the idea as appearing sycophantic. Maybe I'd find something for Luke to read next time he came to stay? I looked at my watch and saw that, as happens to me whenever I'm in a bookstore, I had lost track of time. I had less than ten minutes until my appointment with Milo Franklin.

By walking quickly, but not so quickly as to break into an unseemly sweat, I managed to arrive exactly on time. Alice played her part with an impressive formality that suggested she might yet make a master spy.

"Ms. Prentice—nice to see you again. Please let me introduce Professor Milo Franklin."

No casual Friday, or, I suspected, casual any day for this gentleman. Milo Franklin was wearing a three-piece suit of pale linen, a starched white shirt, and a brown tie. His dress shoes and bald head gleamed as if both had been polished. I held out my hand. "Professor Franklin, I'm Nell Prentice."

He inclined his head and shook my hand. His was unexpectedly rough for an academician—I wondered if he had a hobby or pastime that would account for the texture of his palm. Martha often has tiny pocks in her fingers from quilting—she tells me they are the identifying marks of those who sew. "A pleasure," Professor Franklin said. I found myself wondering whether he and Gabe Chan ever got together for a rousing game of Man of Fewest Words.

Alice said, "The conference room is free, Ms. Prentice, if you and Professor Franklin want to talk there."

I thanked her, and with Professor Franklin beside me walked the short distance to the room where I had conducted my two prior interviews. By this third one I had my opening remarks ready, subject of course to revision as my interviewee's personality revealed itself.

"Professor Franklin," I said, "there are a number of student files missing from the Classics office. Chairman Benson—" my use of the top dog title was deliberate, but drew no reaction that I could see—"has asked me to interview in confidence members of the department to see if anyone has an idea who might have taken them. I saw in the Hathorne catalog that you have the most seniority of any faculty member—you must know this place and the people pretty well."

"Not really," he said. "I don't socialize with other staff in my leisure hours, and I don't invite students to my home for parties." When he said this I tried without success to picture him in his three-piece suit, surrounded by boisterous young people in jeans and flip flops spilling food on his rug. "I engage in those interactions that are expected of me, of course, but it is important to me that my time off be precisely that."

"I can certainly understand that," I said. "As Professor Benson may have told you, the classics are my escape from the work I do—as different as two pursuits can be."

I was flattered to see this man, by his own description uncomfortable with social nuance, look at me with obvious interest. "Yes, Professor Benson did mention that. He said you have a special interest in Herodotus."

I would have loved to get into a discussion of Herodotus as the Father of History versus the Father of Lies with an expert, but I was being paid to solve this case, not engage in interesting side trips. I said, "I do love to read his histories. Whether you believe him or not, he's a wonderful storyteller."

"Who," Professor Franklin said, "cannily tells us quite often that he himself doesn't believe the tale he is about to relate."

"He does!" I said, perilously close to abandoning my resolution to stick to the subject at hand. "When I've been dealing all day with people's problems it puts things in perspective to read that even Croesus wasn't considered the happiest man of his time."

" 'Which I myself do not believe'," Professor Franklin said.

Even as I laughed at his wit I lost no time in seizing upon a good opening. I said, "I suppose it's hard for most people to believe that if they had plenty of money they could still be unhappy. Professor Benson and I were talking about that, in the context of his inherited wealth."

"Alec," Professor Franklin said—was there any significance in this use of his chairman's first name?—"is fortunate in that, and in having the freedom to pursue his career without financial constraints. Though why anyone would choose to be an administrator is beyond me."

"You wouldn't enjoy that part of the job?"

"Not in the least. Anxious undergraduates, hovering parents, the trauma of failing grades. Alec deals with all that on a daily basis so the rest of us can teach."

Hearing this, my best guess was that Professor Franklin wasn't harboring any personal grudge against his department chair. He certainly didn't covet Alec Benson's job for himself. I said, "What about Alice—Ms. Kent? Can you think of any student who might want to get her into trouble?" Or faculty, I thought, but didn't say.

He shook his head. "The students all love her. She keeps cookies on her desk for them, and is a reliable source for the office supplies they're always running out of."

There were cookies I'd missed? By now I was fairly certain that Professor Franklin was not my man, but I was reluctant to end such an interesting interview. I said, "If you don't mind my asking—what are *your* interests in your spare time?"

He smiled, showing small, slightly uneven teeth. "Something appropriately classical, in fact. I'm a potter."

"Really!" I said. That explained the roughened hands. "Do you take the classical motifs as models?"

"No—my designs and colors are quite modern. I like to experiment, try new techniques."

"And do you sell your work?"

"No. I give the more successful pieces as gifts."

There went my chance to case his house for the missing files under the guise of pot-shopping. I said, "Professor Franklin, it's been a real pleasure talking with you. I hope the summer vacation gives you lots of time to work on your pots. Just don't fashion another Pandora—our world has enough troubles."

"Hesiod," he said without hesitation. "Alec's specialty—not mine."

I stopped back at the Classics office to thank Alice and Dr. Benson for their help, and was careful to show no recognition of the name Libby Morse when Alice told me that was who I'd be interviewing Monday. By three I was back in my office, listening to a voice mail message from Terry Burke.

"Nell, could you call me at work as soon as you get this? Russ has a new brainstorm, and if he goes through with it the VA will have no choice but to accept his resignation and fill the job."

I dialed the number she had left—it was the main switchboard number of Higgins and Lathrop. Terry had gone on to explain in her message that she wanted me to get through when I called and not get her voice mail. "Hi, Terry," I said when she came on the line. "What's this about more grief from Russ?"

"Oh, Nell," she said, "he is driving me crazy. This morning just as I was going out the door he told me he couldn't be letting me support him and that tomorrow he was going to apply for a job at McDonald's."

"A great use of his skills and training," I said. "And the salary will easily send your three kids to college. Speaking of the kids, are they home yet?"

"Yes—I just talked to them. I call them every day at this time to make sure they haven't come up with some creative new way of getting around Russ."

"Do this for me, Terry. Call Russ and tell him I'm on my way over there. Say you spoke to me, oh, twenty minutes ago, so he can't go out to avoid talking to me. And tell him"—I was already getting up from my desk, with the phone still in my hand—"I want to talk to the kids. Especially Emmy."

CHAPTER NINETEEN

I made a quick stop for cookies and was ringing the Burkes' doorbell at quarter of four. Matthew answered, showing no recognition of the friend of Mommy's who had given him a battery-powered dinosaur with which Terry later assured me he had driven the whole family around the bend. I beamed at him, clueless as ever at making conversation with someone who only came up to my waist.

"Hi! You're Matthew, right? I came here once before. Are you still in kindergarten? Do you like it?"

He looked at me steadily, out of Terry's big brown eyes, then turned to yell for reinforcements.

"Daddy—a lady's here." Without waiting for a response he turned and walked away.

"I brought cookies," I said to his departing back.

I stepped inside and closed the door, and in a minute Russ appeared, wiping his hands on a dish towel. "Everything got crazy this morning," he said, apparently as an explanation of the dish towel. "But I can rinse out the coffee pot and make some…"

"No, thank you," I said. I held up the bag of cookies that had proved unimpressive to Matthew. "Chocolate chip. For the kids. I bought the kind without nuts in case anybody's allergic."

Actually, I was the cookie aficionada who wanted nothing beyond the perfection of chocolate, sugar, eggs and butter. Chocolate chip purity itself, as long as you didn't consider the additives that would probably keep the cookies edible if they were found in Pompeii.

"That's really nice of you," Russ said. "They get fruit after school so this is a special treat."

I knew it. Away from the alert eyes of her children Terry gobbled M&M's as if they were, well, candy, but at home it was strictly the broad base of the food pyramid.

"Maybe I shouldn't have…" I began, looking around for somewhere to hide the illicit snack before it could undo Terry's healthy regimen for her kids. I found myself looking into Matthew's eyes, and saw his two sisters standing behind him.

"Where are the cookies you brought?" he said.

Russ asked his son what the magic word was, and told all three children to sit at the table for their snack. Emmy spoke up.

"I don't eat cookies. They're totally refined sugar. I've got homework." She turned to leave, her skinny shoulders hunched in a sleeveless dark top. The waistband on her jeans looked to be no more than twelve inches around.

"Emmy," Russ said.

She stopped, somehow managing to hunch her shoulders even further. Russ said, "We have a guest. You don't have to have any of the cookies Ms. Prentice was nice enough to bring, but I want you—all of you—to sit at the table and show some manners. Annabelle, would you get out the milk, and glasses for everybody?"

No two of the glasses Annabelle fetched from the dishwasher were the same. Mine had World's Best Mom written on it. I made sure the children got settled in their rightful chairs before I sat in their mother's place, across from Russ. Matthew took a noisy gulp of milk before turning to his father with a milk mustache. "Can I have three cookies?"

Emmy rolled her eyes. The lower lids looked faintly smudged, as if she might have rubbed off some makeup that, at eleven, she was much too young to be wearing. "You are going to be such a blimp," she said to her brother.

"Emmy," Russ said again. She tossed her hair, dark like her father's, and got up to go to the refrigerator. When she closed the refrigerator door she was holding an apple and clearly about to try again to go back to her room.

"Bring that to the table," Russ said.

Emmy stalked past me, tossing her hair again to show her disdain for all present company. If she were mine, I'd take her for a Marine buzz cut. My nephew Luke, with his own teenaged silences and expressions of boredom, was suddenly looking like the world's most endearing kid.

"No milk," Emmy said, as her father held up the carton. Russ let that one go and turned to his younger daughter. "Annie B?"

She nodded, then said to me, "Chocolate chip cookies are my favorite."

Already catching on to the family dynamics, I gave Annabelle a smile that was not so effusive as to bring forth jealous sarcasm from her sister. She must be six now—a round-faced little girl in a dress printed with flowers. Two takers for my offering. Three if you counted me, and I was a sure thing.

We sat at the table, or slouched in Emmy's case, while two of the children talked about school. Russ cut in with practiced skill just as Matthew was about to relate what Jason said the cafeteria dessert looked like. ("Not at the table, Mattie—you can tell me later.") Matthew reached for another cookie, his fourth by my surreptitious count, as Annabelle began talking about getting to play a bell in music class. They were cute kids, with their mother's outgoing personality—fun to be around. But perversely, I found myself drawn to Emmy, whose only contribution to the gathering had been crunching on her apple. I remembered being that age, feeling unlovable and doing every obnoxious thing I could to see that my parents got that message. Not that they ever did, of course.

There was something else, too, that made it easy for me to tolerate Emmy's churlish behavior. I also remembered how it felt to have a child's crush on a kind grownup. But this child had had her heart broken by Oliver's death and was at an age when she was likely to hold her pain inside.

She was getting up from the table now, leaving her apple core next to the unused milk glass. Russ said, "Put that in the sink, please. Do you want to talk to Ms. Prentice here, or in your room?"

I admired the way he put the question, giving his daughter a choice, though not the choice I was sure she wanted—that of not talking to me at all. Emmy picked up the apple core and took it to the sink, then spoke with her back to me.

"Whatever," she said.

I spoke up then, wanting to take advantage of an option that would give me privacy to talk to Russ's daughter without his overhearing. "Emmy? Could we talk in your room?"

By way of answer she walked out of the kitchen and I followed, turning to give Russ a quick and I hoped reassuring smile. His lips were parted as if he'd been about to say something about Emmy's exasperating behavior, and I hoped my smile would convey that I hadn't noticed a thing. He looked uncertain, then shook his head and turned back to his two children who, for the moment, thought that Daddy was someone to actually be listened to.

I had no trouble telling which room was Emmy's—the sign on the partly opened door said PRIVATE! KEEP OUT! I tapped on the door, got a mumble in response, and stepped inside. With a girl I suppose I was expecting a feminine look, but Emmy's room was as plainly decorated and disordered as Luke's dorm room. Emmy herself was sitting in her desk chair next to an unmade bed with several stuffed animals tangled in the blue machine-stitched quilt. I thought of Martha's beautiful needlework, her serene personality, and had a momentary fantasy of delivering Emmy to Martha for a month or so and getting the child back wreathed in smiles, showing off her new maidenly skills. Right.

"Is it OK if I sit on your bed?" I asked Emmy. She shrugged. I moved aside a bright green stuffed turtle and a gray dolphin and made myself as comfortable as I could on the low bed. Over my head and on one wall were posters of boy performers, none of whom looked much older than Emmy. I'd like to be able to say that at this age I had precociously adorned my room with a bust of Cicero, but in truth I opened my eyes at the beginning of my second decade to a glossy publicity still of the entire Walton clan.

"Emmy," I said, knowing better than to try a ploy like pretending an interest in the child rock stars, "I want to talk to you about Oliver."

I thought she wasn't going to respond, but then she said, without looking at me, "He's dead. Do you get that?"

"Yes, I get that," I said, hearing the pain in her sullen voice. "But your Mom says you and he were good friends. I never got to meet him—can you tell me what he was like?"

CHAPTER TWENTY

From my very brief acquaintance with Miss Emmy Burke, I was prepared for the shrug, no answer, something mumbled and unintelligible. But she said, "He was cool, OK? He didn't treat me like a little kid."

I took the hint, whether or not she had meant it as such. "Then I won't treat you that way, either."

She was turned half away from me, but now she gave me a very quick look of surprise. I said, "Your mother came to me for help. She and your Dad don't want you worrying, but you probably know a lot more than they think you do."

This time, she nodded, ever so slightly. I proceeded as carefully as if she were a feral cat that had just taken a cautious step in my direction. "Your mother told me your father quit his job because of Oliver. I'm trying to figure out why he would think what happened was his fault."

Emmy didn't respond to my implied question. Maybe she couldn't. She said, "Oliver was teaching me to play the guitar. He said I was getting good, and that he'd talk to my Mom and Dad about getting me a guitar of my own."

I wondered where Oliver's guitar was now. If his mother didn't want it, what a lot it would probably mean to this little girl. I said, "What kind of songs did you play?"

The shrug. "Just songs. Like Down in the Valley. He showed me how to do a seventh chord."

"That's great," I said. "I'd love to hear you play sometime."

Her face closed up, just like that. I must have sounded as if I were trying to be part of what she'd had with Oliver. I changed tack, keeping the focus on how I was asking for her help because she'd been special to Oliver. "Before Oliver died did he seem sad? Did he talk to you about anything that might be bothering him?"

Her expression changed again—she was considering my questions. "There was this one time—he sounded like he was crying, but he said he wasn't, that it was just that..."

She stopped, and I gave her a moment. "Just that what, Emmy? Please—help me figure out what's going on with your Dad."

Emmy looked past me, toward the posters of the boy rock stars. I prayed she wasn't going to cry herself—I wouldn't get another word out of her if that happened. But Terry Burke's daughter was a tough kid.

"He said..." she paused, then it came out in a rush, "...that it was just getting to him because of somebody who wasn't any older than me."

I waited to see if she was going to say more. When she didn't, I said, "Thank you, Emmy. Is that the word he used—somebody?"

"He said 'she'. She wasn't any older than me." She was upset now, and I could see the gleam of tears in her eyes. I said again, "Thank you. For telling me that. I think Oliver was really lucky to have you for a friend."

The tears were about to fall, and I knew she wouldn't want me to see her crying. I got up off her bed and went to the door. "Do you want this closed?"

She nodded. I stepped into the hallway and shut the door quietly behind me.

Russ was in the kitchen, peeling potatoes while his two younger children sat at the counter, chattering away. It was impossible to look at their open, animated faces and imagine that in just a few years it would be their turn for the miseries of adolescence. I said hello to them, and then spoke to their father.

"Russ, I need to talk to you about something. Are Matthew and Annabelle allowed to watch television?"

The children turned startled, hopeful expressions on me, then on their father. "Please, Daddy?" Annabelle said. "Can we put on PBS?"

Exactly what I had in mind. Some animated creatures with high-pitched voices to divert these two and cover the conversation I needed to have with their father. Russ said, "Just for a few minutes while Ms. Prentice and I talk. And not too loud."

Annabelle and Matthew sprang down from the kitchen stools and sprinted for the living room. The TV came on, and I crossed to the counter and took one of the stools.

"So," said Russ, "Isn't Emmy a joy these days? Don't get me wrong—she's a terrific kid. I just wish she wasn't hitting the teenaged bumps quite so early. Did you get her to talk to you at all?"

"As a matter of fact, yes," I said. "She told me about the guitar lessons, and about Oliver not treating her like a kid." Russ had stopped what he was doing and was watching me with the potato peeler still raised in his hand. "And how about this, Russ? He told her about somebody who wasn't any older than your daughter, and who apparently made him cry when he thought about her."

Russ went a guilty shade of pale. I pressed my advantage as unequivocally as I could.

"Who, Russ? Who was this girl he told Emmy—and I'm sure you—about?"

CHAPTER TWENTY ONE

Russ was shaking his head, for what reason I wasn't sure. I said, "Russ? What did he tell you?"

"There are confidentiality requirements," he said. "I could never do my job if the patients thought they couldn't trust me not to repeat what they tell me."

I refrained from pointing out that at present he wasn't doing his job at all. I said, "Tell me this, then. Had Oliver done anything criminal, hurt a little girl he couldn't stop thinking about?"

"No," Russ said. "Absolutely nothing like that." He drew in a breath. "The ethics can get pretty complicated when things happen in a war zone, but what Oliver saw, what sent him over the edge, was nothing compared to the things I hear from other veterans. But everybody's got his breaking point, and that was his."

"Russ," I said, "your friend, Emmy's friend, is gone. If he didn't do anything wrong then you're not hurting him or his mother by telling me what he told you. The only ones being hurt now are you and your family, and I can't believe Oliver would ever want that."

Russ shook his head again, but not in a negative way. More as if to clear it. From the living room came the shrill, bubbly soundtrack of children's television.

"The thing that made it all the worse," Russ said, "was that it was their last night there. Oliver and his buddies were being rotated back to the States the next day."

Russ walked to the kitchen window. He stared out for a minute, then came over and took the stool next to me. He said, "Oliver told me this story in bits and pieces, when he started to trust me. I'll see if I can put it all together for you, the way he told it.

"He said the celebrating started early and went on all night—the kind of hell raising you'd expect from guys who had been living for months in danger and were hours from saying goodbye to it all. Oliver wasn't much of a drinker, which was maybe why he was the first to pass out from the fifth of vodka the group was passing around. They were gathered in the mess hall, with the lights out, and when somebody noticed Oliver, eyes closed, slumped against the wall, there was an argument about what to do with him. Carrying him back to the barracks would be much too likely to attract attention, so his buddies arranged Oliver's unconscious body in the pantry that adjoined the kitchen. So that he wouldn't wake up and fall down the basement stairs, they closed and locked the pantry door."

Russ paused, shaking his head. "That was beyond stupid. He could have vomited and choked. But they were all way too drunk to be thinking straight.

"Oliver woke up in a place that was pitch-black. He pulled himself up along the wall and felt the surface until his hand touched a light switch. When the lights came on something made a high, squeaking sound, like a rat.

"He told me the base was lousy with rats. The cats couldn't keep up with them. He looked around for where the sound was coming from and saw a person, a kid, hiding under a shelf.

"She must have been in the kitchen when she heard this rowdy gang of drunks coming. The whole time they were there, getting more and more raucous, she must have been getting more terrified. Then the door opened, Oliver's buddies dragged him inside, and she was locked in the dark with a strange man.

"When Oliver realized the sound he'd heard was coming from a child he just started by instinct to go to her. There was no farther back for her to go, but she tried, letting go of what she'd been clutching. It rolled toward Oliver and landed at his feet.

"It was one of those giant government-issue cans of stewed tomatoes. Christ knows how she thought she was going to carry it or open it, but it was food."

I interrupted at this point with a question I needed to ask. "Russ, did Oliver do something to hurt that little girl? Maybe not even remembering until later..."

Russ glared at me. "I already told you no. You have no idea what it's like, what we send these kids into. Some of them start out with personality problems and they can be the ones to snap, especially when there's drinking and drugs. But not Oliver. And never with a kid."

"I'm sorry," I said. "You're right—I don't know what it's like."

Russ took a minute before resuming the story. "He said the high from the booze went right out of him, seeing that kid with a goddamn can of tomatoes that was almost as big as she was. He tried to tell her it was all right, she could keep the food, he'd get her more, but she either didn't know any English or she was too scared to listen to what he was saying. So he gave up, and pounded on the pantry door until his buddies heard him. The second they opened that door the kid was out of there like a demon was chasing her.

"Oliver's buddies were trying to calm him down, telling him he was going to get them all in trouble, but they couldn't stop him from picking up that tin can that was still on the floor and sending it all the way across the room and through a window."

Russ was breathing a little hoarsely. I said, "We're safe at home, and we send them into that."

It had never been any different, of course. For all its violence and brutality the Iliad would be rated "R" today. But Hector and Achilles, if they ever existed, were dead three thousand years. What Oliver had seen was happening today, all around the world.

As if thinking along the same lines as I was Russ said, "The war is one thing. People with weapons are trying to kill us and we're trying to kill them. You have to hope most soldiers believe they're on the right side. But Oliver said it never hit him before that we were really making war on kids with empty bellies."

"So when he got back he couldn't adjust?"

"A lot of them can't. Getting them to even admit they need help can be the hardest part. Oliver had all the symptoms of PTSD—night after night of insomnia, then nightmares when he did sleep. Depression, drinking. But with all of it he was such a good person. I trusted him completely with my kids. I should have been able to help him."

"So, that's it," I said. "You lost a patient and a friend—a good person—and now everybody depending on you has to pay the price?"

"Where do you get off?" he said angrily, then glanced at the door to the living room and lowered his voice. "I know you're Terry's friend and we both appreciate what you did to have the reward money go to her, but this is my family and I'll take care of it."

"By hiding from what's happened? By denying your other patients the help they need?"

"I can't help them!" he said. "I've lost whatever I had that let me step back and be objective." He got up from the stool and turned away. "I don't want to talk to you anymore. Please go. I'll tell Terry you gave it a try, but this is something you can't fix."

I stayed where I was until he had to turn and face me. When he did I said, "Just one more question, Russ, and then I'll go. Is this what Oliver would want?"

"You didn't know him—I did."

"You're right. But I feel like I knew him. I wish I had. A man who felt things and cared about the misery in the world. Who cared about your family. Would that man want to bring trouble to your family by the decision he made? Would he want to keep those other wounded soldiers, the ones who are here and waiting for your help, from getting it?"

I got off the kitchen stool and went to where Russ was standing. I put a hand on his arm.

"Give it another try. You're not going to win every one—none of us do—but get back there to those guys who need you. And when you do see somebody you've helped walk out of the hospital able to live his or her life, tell yourself you did it for Oliver."

Terry called me at home at nine o'clock that evening. "I wanted to wait until the kids were in bed and Russ and I finished talking. Nell, I don't know how to thank you. Russ is going in on Monday—he says he'll see how it goes, but I know that man. Once he's there and helping people he'll remember that this is what he wants to do. There isn't enough money in the world to pay you for this but I've never been this happy to be writing a check. Just tell me the amount to fill in."

"Tell you what, Terry," I said. I moved my hand with the phone in it so that Woody, who had jumped up on the phone table just in case the call was for him, could sniff at the receiver. "You and Russ decide what's a fair amount and then donate it in Oliver's memory. Maybe to one of those places that feeds the hungry. Russ will have some ideas."

"You are something," Terry said.

"What's more," I told her, "let's not forget about that swanky lunch I owe you. We'll get gussied up and have martinis and shrimp cocktails to start. Or—maybe this is an even better idea—we'll pick a place that is too cool for words and the three of us can go. You, me, and Emmy."

CHAPTER TWENTY TWO

On Saturday I slept a little later than usual and woke up feeling elated all over again. A friend had come to me for help, and I had been able to give her just that. I opened my bedroom door to a sunny morning, with Woody stretched out in the kitchen window. I fed him while my coffee brewed, then took mug and cat back to bed and picked up the mystery I had been reading. It was set in Scandinavia, in winter, and I enjoyed my coffee even more in the fictional atmosphere of snow and wind and isolated farmhouses.

I met Tom for lunch at Brigham's, where normally I would top off my meal with ice cream, but my sweet tooth was still sated from my birthday. We sat in a booth with our iced tea and sandwiches, talking about the week just past—he was glad to hear that things had turned out well with Terry and her family. When he reached for the check I put my hand over his.

"We're splitting this. My birthday was wonderful, but it's over for another year and I'm back to paying my own way."

"An independent woman," Tom said, accepting the ten-dollar bill I held out to him. "If you ever do agree to marry me I suppose you'll want to buy your own ring."

"Sure. That way I could bypass your good taste and go for something oversized and tacky." This was how we bantered back and forth on the subject of the "M" word. He wasn't really asking me, I wasn't really needing to give the subject any serious thought.

"Here comes our waitress," I said, probably sounding rescued. "It's my turn to leave the tip."

The day was a little too warm for the jacket Luke had sent me, but I'd brought it anyway, looped around my waist. Tom had on the gray sweater I'd given him for Christmas. We walked hand in hand through the Public Garden in companionable silence, passing the colorful flowerbeds and the swan boats and the new babies bundled up for their Spring outings. I felt very content, as if I could get used to this, especially since Tom would be coming home with me.

Back at my place, I made dinner for us while Tom sat at the table with Woody in his lap, reading the Boston *Globe* he'd picked up while we were in town. He'd never uttered a word of complaint about my apartment having no television and few books to read that weren't thousands of years old. But of course we were only together for a night at a time, then it was back to our own places, his with cable. What if he did ask, and I said yes? We'd need a bigger apartment than either of us had now. Would he have the guys over to watch football? Would he want a dog? Where would all my books go?

Just then the spaghetti sauce began to boil over. I lowered the heat under the pot and put out of my mind all thoughts of marriage and its myriad complications. If Tom did propose, and I accepted, that would be the time for me to begin obsessing in earnest about the million problematic details of sharing a home with another person.

My doubts and reservations notwithstanding, it was nice to wake up next to Tom on Sunday morning. It was raining—I listened to the peaceful sound as I made a big pot of coffee and got bagels out of the freezer to defrost in the microwave. Tom was having lunch at his mother's and reminded me that I was very much included in the invitation. "Sheila would love to see you," he said, spreading a bagel with the homemade blueberry jam Miles and Tilda, Luke's other family, had sent from Maine. I knew that was true. Sheila Kramer had no reservations at all about whether her son and I should get married and, as Tom had once said, give her a step cat. She probably already had a mother-of-the-groom dress hanging in her closet.

"You know I'd love to," I said, getting up from the table and kissing the top of his head as I passed behind him. "But laundry and cat care duties and bill-paying call. And in between doing all that I need to prepare for an interview I'm doing tomorrow. Give Sheila my love, and tell her I want to take her to lunch very soon."

After Tom left I showered and cleaned up the kitchen and went down to the basement to put in a load of laundry. I returned to find Woody waiting by my reading chair for my undivided attention.

"Come on up," I said to him, repositioning the Hathorne catalog I'd taken from my desk. "Make yourself comfortable, and we'll see what we can find out about Professor Libby Morse."

Elizabeth Lyman Morse had a bachelor's degree from Smith and a PhD in Classics from Yale. In her photo, she was pictured not in a conventional office setting but apparently mountain climbing. Next to the photo was a list of publications, honors, and memberships in organizations advancing the interests of women educators.

"An overachiever," I said to Woody. "Do you think she'll approve of me, the only female private investigator listed in the Boston Yellow Pages?"

Woody yawned, and tucked one languid paw over the other. He is an underachiever of the first magnitude, and I wouldn't have it any other way.

CHAPTER TWENTY THREE

Professor Benson and Libby Morse were already in the conference room when I arrived at Hathorne the next day for my appointment. Alice walked me there and tapped on the open door before gesturing me to follow her inside. Professor Benson stood as we entered the room, but Libby Morse remained seated, her hands folded on the table. Only when Professor Benson said, "Ms. Prentice, this is Professor Morse" did she stand to shake my hand.

Libby Morse was of average height, but she had presence. Her white hair had to be premature—I knew from the catalog information that she was only in her early fifties. Her short, feathery haircut, suitable for rock climbing as well as for disdaining female vanity, framed her angular face and set off her very unusual eyes—one green and one brown. She wore a navy blue pantsuit, white blouse, simple earrings, and no makeup.

"I'm pleased to meet you, Professor," I said, returning her firm handshake. "Thank you for taking the time to talk to me."

As Alec Benson walked to the door, he said to Professor Morse, "We'll talk more about your ideas for restructuring the honors seminar, Libby. You've given me lots to think about." Before Alice preceded him out the door she asked, "Could I get anyone coffee?"

I was about to accept, again more for the social ritual than for the coffee itself, when Professor Morse said, "No, thank you, Alice. If Ms. Prentice or I want tea or coffee we'll go to the faculty lounge."

I suspected her response would have been considerably more acerbic had Professor Benson been the one offering the services of his secretary. Alice nodded and they both went out, Professor Benson closing the conference room door behind him. Libby Morse sat back down, at the head of the conference table, and I took the chair to her right.

"Did Professor Benson tell you why I'm interviewing members of the Classics Department?" I began.

"Student records." She had a clipped way of speaking, like someone who might once have had to overcome an unwanted accent. "Not where they should be, and therefore subject to misuse."

"Can you give me any help with who might have taken the records?"

She looked at me for a moment before replying. Up close, the different-colored eyes were even more arresting. "I don't concern myself with the office filing system." Which was hardly what I had asked. "Alice seems to do a very adequate job of managing all that." A thought seemed to occur to her. "I hope no one is thinking of trying that one—blame the girl."

The way she bit off the word "girl" made it clear what she thought of that demeaning usage. A not unexpected reaction from what I'd heard about this woman, but I was far more interested in the implication that she would not want to see Alice in any trouble. As I thought about it, that, too, made sense. It must be common knowledge in the department that *a man* had done Alice dirt, with no consequences. (I was still seething about that myself, on general principles.) I tried another tack.

"I heard Professor Benson say you have some ideas on an honors seminar."

She raised her eyebrows, dark in contrast to her hair. The gesture widened her striking eyes. "Yes, I have quite a few ideas. But since most of them involve change none ever seem to reach the level of actual implementation."

"None?" I repeated. She gave me a sharp look. I couldn't tell whether it was a look of annoyance, or one of approval that I would challenge her.

"Few, then. Very few. But I am persistent. I did gain department approval last year to coordinate with the drama department a production of *Lysistrata*."

And what a lead you would have made, I thought. Aristophanes' splendid looser of armies, pitting strong women against foolish, militaristic men. I said, "I wish I'd seen it. Does the department vote on new proposals?"

"Committees," she said, in a tone that drove a stake through the heart of that word. "To get them on her side, a woman usually seems to need extra effort and preparation. I suppose you find the same thing in your profession."

She was talking, on the subject I wanted her on, and I knew I should just nod in agreement. But I felt compelled to defend the many men who had given me a helping hand as I learned my way around the profession I took up when my husband Michael died. I said, " Some of my colleagues have been great. There are always a few of the other kind, of course, the ones who want to see a woman fail out of their own jealousy or insecurity, but I don't let those get to me."

"It may be different in a college environment," she said. "So few positions, so many applicants. Many of my female colleagues seem to want to protect themselves by staying in the background, as if they should be grateful to have a job at all, however much they've worked for it. I can't be like that."

"So how do you go about it?" I asked. "How do you present your ideas for changing the way things are done?"

She seemed to warm to my question, as if pleased to be asked. "First, I do all the groundwork I can. I research costs—that all-important factor—level of student interest, the possibility of grants, and anything else that will make my case. After that, I go to my department chair and ask for his support."

"And is Professor Benson generally supportive of your proposals?"

"Alec has an open mind. He's one of the few here who do. The rest of them pay lip service to the value of change and innovation, but I suspect one or two of them would be just as happy if women had never gotten the vote."

"What about your *Lysistrata* production? Was Professor Benson with you on that?"

"He was," Libby Morse said. "He was enthusiastic about a project that could use the classics to inspire today's young women."

"Professor Morse," I said, "Here's the concern I have. Whoever took those records may have as a motive embarrassing Professor Benson. If there was serious misuse of the records he might even lose his job. Can you think of anyone who might want to see that happen?"

She looked at me with those distracting eyes, and it occurred to me that I hadn't once seen her smile. "Ms. Prentice, I can't speak for anyone but myself. I would not want to see Alec step down and be replaced by any of the likely candidates. Alec can be a little more immured in tradition than I might like, but he treats all staff members, male and female, equally. The Department could, and would, do much worse if Alec were to leave."

She looked at her watch then, and I remembered Alice telling me that Professor Morse was going out of town right after our interview. I said, "Thank you for your help. I won't keep you any longer. I hope you have a good vacation."

"Thank you," Libby Morse said. "Actually, I only take a week off before my summer project. I'm involved in tutoring New Haven girls from poor families who show promise but aren't on an equal footing competing with boys for college scholarships."

"You're very committed," I said.

"Thank you," she said again. "I'm also a realist. By the time most Hathorne girls arrive here, after a decade of riding lessons and summer camp and trips to Europe, it's not easy to interest them in possibilities other than marriage and motherhood." She smiled then, for the first time. "The other girls—they remind me of myself at that age."

I felt flattered that this woman, obviously a private person, would confide in me such a personal fact. I was also relieved that while Libby Morse might not be a wholly uncritical fan of Professor Benson, it was clear that she had no reason to sabotage his job, or Alice's. We shook hands, and she left the conference room. I took a moment to gather my things, and found Alice waiting when I stepped into the corridor.

"I didn't want to interrupt, Ms. Prentice," she said, "but Professor Benson wanted to be sure you didn't leave without stopping by his office. There's someone he wants you to meet."

We walked side by side down the corridor and went into the outer office. I heard Professor Benson's voice coming through the open door, and a second voice. Alice looked in, then gestured for me. Professor Benson stood as I came in and indicated a stout woman in a red suit who turned in the visitor chair to look at me.

"Ms. Prentice, come in. Our visiting classicist," he said to the woman, cueing me in that he had sketched out some kind of cover story to explain my presence at Hathorne. "Ms. Prentice, may I present Mrs. Henrietta Greenberg."

CHAPTER TWENTY FOUR

With Libby Morse I had assumed she was making a point when she remained seated for a moment before standing to greet me. Henrietta Greenberg didn't get up at all, which meant I had to go to her and reach down, as if doing homage, to offer my hand.

"A pleasure," she said, her white hand covered with rings limp in my clasp. Everything about her—the styled, frosted hair, the red suit, the designer handbag—spoke of money. Not how I would picture a woman with grown grandchildren. She had a small, trembly chin and, under the carefully applied makeup, a look of discontent, or possibly distrust.

Professor Benson said, "Mrs. Greenberg and her late husband are among Hathorne's most generous benefactors." That use of "late" always struck me oddly, as if the decedent were the White Rabbit, hustling along on his rabbit paws, exclaiming as he consulted his pocket watch. I don't know of a better word, though. Maybe somebody could come up with a neologism from the Greek *chronios*, which sounds as if it means "out of time."

"...around here?" Mrs. Greenberg's voice, slightly tremulous, rose more than is customary to indicate a question. Damn—I'd missed something. To my relief, Professor Benson stepped adroitly into the awkward moment, providing a further cue as to who I was supposed to be.

"I've been telling Mrs. Greenberg how you came to one of my lectures and I found out you were a classicist yourself." He smiled, his charm even more evident in the face of Mrs. Greenberg's dour expression. "I'll let you tell the rest."

"Do you teach?" Mrs. Greenberg asked, in a peremptory way as if interviewing for a new parlor maid and asking about her ironing skills. Professor Benson was watching me, still smiling, but looking a little uneasy about whether I was up to this improvisational challenge. I tried to convey to him by my confident tone that he was about to witness my skill at being *splendide mendax*, which is Latin for full of it.

"Actually," I said, "I don't have a degree. I read a lot on my own, and go to lectures like Professor Benson's—" I smiled at him "—and I take a few courses."

"At what institutions? My husband was very interested in the classics—some of the best scholars in our city knew him."

"The University of Massachusetts," I said, and saw the interest leave her face. No hobnobbing for the Greenbergs with the enrollees of a state school situated next door to a housing project.

"My husband," Mrs. Greenberg said again, in that keeper-of-the-flame manner of some widows, "was so fond of Hathorne, and dear Alec." She simpered at Professor Benson, her little chin bobbing, and he gallantly inclined his head to her. I thought of Milo Franklin and how he'd blow this unpalatable part of an administrator's job the first time out. "No doubt Alec has told you—" she nodded at me, who was not "dear" anybody, or even possessed of a name—"that in addition to his financial generosity my husband acquired for the college a very special piece of art, didn't he, Alec?"

"Yes," Professor Benson said. He sounded as if he had a fish bone caught in his throat. I had a wild thought that she might be about to ask him to show me the manuscript, which was supposedly safely stored just a few yards away.

"A manuscript," she went on. "Lucretius. It's extremely valuable—from the Vatican. Not," she added quickly, "that we're Catholic."

I had a satisfying moment of feeling superior to Henrietta Greenberg. She might be wearing more money on her fingers than I made in years, but I knew and she didn't that the real Machiavelli Lucretius was priceless, and would no more be in the Classics office of a small college in Boston than would the Mona Lisa.

"Alec takes special care of my husband's gift." Again she gave Professor Benson a coy look, as if confident he found her charming. "Only once a year is it taken out of there…" she actually looked toward the rare book room, and I heard Professor Benson draw in his breath. "In fact, Ms——Price, is it?—if the classics interest you, you have a unique opportunity. My husband's gift is displayed at graduation, when I present the scholarship named for him." Now she turned the debatable charm on me, the lady-of-the-manor graciously taking notice of an underling. "Graduation is in just a few weeks. I want you to be there to see for yourself the treasure my Clayton"—apparently Mr. Greenberg's first name—"left for all of us to remember him by."

Before I could respond she lifted her wrist to look at a tiny, bejeweled watch. "Heavens, is that the time? I have another engagement." She stood, and Alec Benson nearly leaped to his feet, no doubt eager to put as much space as possible between Henrietta Greenberg and the rare book room. She pulled on a long, silky pair of gloves while I tried to remember the last time I'd seen anyone wearing gloves that weren't from L.L. Bean. "So," she said to me, foregoing any attempt at my name, "shall we be seeing you at the awards ceremony?"

"Mrs. Greenberg," I said, concealing my pleasure at the difference in our heights now that she was standing, " I can assure you, nothing would please me more."

CHAPTER TWENTY FIVE

For the following week, as the New England Spring advanced, I interviewed the rest of the Hathorne Classics staff, with frustratingly little to show for it. My instinct for knowing when someone is lying is pretty well developed, but none of my meetings with faculty, staff, and graduate students triggered that instinct. I learned that Alec Benson was intelligent/ fair/ a real motivator, and that Alice Kent was a pleasure to work with (the general consensus of the men) or a model of female survival and pluck (two of the women). I relished the opportunity to talk with and learn from each of these specialists in the Classics, but graduation was now only three weeks away, and I had not a clue who had taken the manuscript or—a constant, nagging worry—whether it was being properly preserved.

Once my interviews at Hathorne were finished, I was able to spend more time in my office working on other cases—calling and emailing people, tracking all manner of personal and even financial information on the Internet. It's just amazing to me what people "post" online where everybody and anybody can see it. It's all a godsend to an investigator who can sit comfortably in her office sipping coffee while she collects information its subject may not want collected. I ended the work week by spending Friday morning doing surveillance of a house whose occupant was claiming disability from a fishy-looking workplace injury scenario. She never appeared, I drank too much coffee, got hot sitting in my car, and at noon gave up for the day. I stopped for lunch at Burger King and drove to my office, deliciously cool now that the air conditioner was working. I was billing my surveillance hours to the appropriate client, the insurance company I once worked for, when the phone rang.

"Nell?" said a familiar voice with a question mark in it.

"Harry! I was thinking of you and the boys a little while ago. I had lunch at their favorite place—Burger King. How are they? How are all of you?"

I met Harry Marcus and his twin boys, Monroe and Madison, when Harry hired me to find his missing wife. I did find Kris Marcus, but not in time. One of my cases that, like Richard III's ghosts, float before me on the edge of sleep, reminding me that we have to keep trying to make things come out right, but sometimes they just don't.

"We're fine," Harry said. "Madison is still excited about singing and wants to know how soon he can audition for *American Idol*, and Monroe thinks he wants to be an Olympic snowboarder like that kid with the red hair."

I had seen Harry and his boys at Christmas. Shy Madison's newfound gift for singing had transformed him. I could picture him in front of the dazzled judges (they'd better be), and me phoning in votes until my fingers were ready to fall off.

"Here's an idea," I said. "Madison can sing the national anthem when Monroe wins the gold medal. No harm in aiming high."

Harry laughed. I waited for him to say more, then prompted him, as I usually had to do. "And you, Harry? How are you?"

"Well," he said, making the word an interjection rather than an adjective. "Remember how I was looking for just the right person to be with the boys after Lisa went back to school?" Lisa was Monroe and Madison's aunt, their mother's sister. "I did find somebody. Stephanie. She's older than the kids I interviewed but can keep up with my guys, and she's really patient. It's worked out great."

I didn't think he could be calling me to chat about satisfactory child care arrangements. I said, "And?"

"Well, here's the thing, Nell." He paused, and I waited. This Stephanie probably had need of her store of patience in dealing with Harry as well as with two almost six-year-olds.

"Stephanie and I"—it came out in a rush—"We're getting married."

The first thought I had was: is this about the boys? But I'm socially programmed. "Harry, that's great!" I said. "Congratulations!"

"Thanks. She's really a wonderful lady. She knows I want the boys to always remember their mother, and she talks to them about Kris even though she didn't know Kris—gets them to talk, really. Monroe still gets moody sometimes and doesn't want to talk but Stephanie knows what he's like and just lets him take his time."

I had lots of questions. How old was "older"? Would there be children or even grandchildren for Madison and Monroe to get used to? But I shouldn't be acting like an investigator here, entitled at least in my own mind to ask question after probing question. Harry's call to me with his news must mean he thought of me as a friend. I said, "When's the wedding?"

"Two weeks from today. The twenty-seventh. It's going to be at Stephanie's place." I remembered Harry's cramped house, which could never hold even a small party of wedding guests. "We're hoping the weather's good—Stephanie has a nice yard." He hesitated again. "Lisa will be there, but not Lorraine and Vic."

I had met Harry's parents-in-law when I was looking for their daughter. After Lorraine and Vic Bennett understood that Harry had nothing to do with their daughter's death, they were able to reconnect with their son-in-law and grandchildren. I said, "Are you disappointed about that?"

"No, no," he said, so quickly that I thought he must be trying to convince himself. "I talked to Vic—he says they're both happy for me, but Lorraine just can't be there. She'd be thinking about Kris, naturally, and doesn't want to spoil things, especially for the boys."

"Get lots of pictures," I said. "Everybody loves pictures of little boys dressed up for a wedding, but grandmothers will walk for miles showing them to complete strangers."

I didn't ask about Harry's own father. I had met Harold Marcus, Senior, almost a year ago during my search for Kris. He and his son were bitterly estranged, and Harold, Senior—Hank—was dying of cancer.

"So it's going to be pretty small," Harry said. "Maybe twenty people. Stephanie's my age," (There was that question answered) "and was married before, but I really want it to be nice for her. The thing is, Nell, I wondered if you could come."

"Yes," I said, without a glance at my calendar. "Thank you, Harry. I'll be there."

"And bring somebody, of course. That is, if..."

"There is," I said. "Somebody." I realized as I replied that might not have been his question. "I'll call him as soon as we're off the phone."

"OK, great. I'll tell Stephanie to get an invitation in the mail to you. It has the time and directions."

After we hung up I sat back in my chair, thinking that for all the calls that bring woes and trouble, some calls like the one I'd just received make the day brighter. I dialed Tom's office and left a message for him, then went to work rescheduling the appointments listed for Harry's wedding day.

CHAPTER TWENTY SIX

was two weeks past my forty-third birthday, with just over two weeks remaining until the Hathorne graduation, when I got a call from California.

"Ms. Prentice?" said a voice that sounded familiar, though I couldn't immediately place it. "It's Jon Halloran."

"Jon," I said, momentarily pleased, then guilty. I hadn't spoken to this man since the few hours we'd spent together six months ago. Why would a cop from California be calling me unless he'd somehow found out what I'd done the one time we'd met? Unless he knew that I'd met up with a gangster named Eliot Wyman, gave him a pass for his part in my brother's death, and handed over a valuable sculpture that didn't belong to him. All to protect Luke, the son of my murdered brother.

"How are you?" I said, projecting innocence and purity of heart across the time zones. "Are you police commissioner yet?"

Jon Halloran laughed. "I'd last a week. The whole country has budget problems, but the way things are going here the next step for the Golden State will be to start printing its own money."

"With Schwarzenegger on it," I said. "In a body builder pose—like Atlas." I stopped right there—maybe Jon Halloran was an avid fan of the Terminator Governor, who had surprised a lot of people when he ran for and won the highest office in a state which, with earthquakes, forest fires, budget nightmares, and endemic loopiness, could have had as its motto "If it isn't one thing it's another." I firmly forbade my mind from turning the phrase into Latin.

"Please," Jon said. "One thing you can always say for this state is that there are knockout women on every corner. Angelina Jolie or Scarlett

Johansson or plenty of others would look great on that thousand-dollar bill we're going to need soon to buy a bag of groceries." Then, in answer to my initial question, he said, "I'm good, Ms. Prentice. Working steady, no new ulcers that I know about. How's your friend doing—the one who called me?"

When I made my trip to California six months ago, I had to leave Tom in the hospital. He'd had a heart attack. I think Tom understood why—because of Luke—I needed to get answers about my brother's death, but that didn't keep him from hating the fact that he was temporarily imprisoned in the country of the sick. It seemed to help that even from a hospital bed he could cut through police red tape for me, including tape strung on the other side of the country.

"Tom is fine," I said. "We're together. And Jon, it's Nell."

"Nell," Jon said. Then, "Did you see today's news?"

I don't watch the news, though I can't escape the headlines that vie for my attention when I log onto my email. Usually they concern, with equal emphasis, standoffs in the Middle East or North Korea, and celebrity news about the shocking demise of some starlet's twenty-seven day marriage. "No," I said. "What's happened?"

"An arrest," Jon said, with obvious levity. "A very solid one, I might add, of somebody we've been after for a long time."

"Congratulations." What could this have to do with me?

"The scuzzball—sorry, the alleged perpetrator—is a guy named Eliot Wyman."

I kept my response as brief as possible. Jon might be a pro at detecting strain in a voice that was lying by omission. "What's the story?"

"Wyman's been running a major drug racket for years, but he's been too high up and too powerful for us to turn the bit players when we got our hands on them. But not this time."

"Why not this time?" I asked.

"Sex," Jon said.

I considered this. There couldn't be much, however sordid, that wasn't available for a price to a man like Wyman. But then I thought of where a lot of people without much in the way of standards draw the line.

"Let me guess," I said. "Girls not too many years past playing Barbie."

"Close," Jon said. "Boys. In particular, a boy whose godfather worked for Wyman. The guy had probably shut his eyes to a million things, but lucky for us, not this time."

So the Furies, who never rest, had finally swooped down on Eliot Wyman. I said, "Well, congratulations, Jon. You guys must be celebrating."

He didn't say anything, and that's when I knew. This call, about a criminal I had supposedly never heard of, had something to do with me. Very much so.

"The thing is," Jon said, "there are photos."

In the context of our conversation, this detail hardly came as a surprise.

"Everything we needed was on the computers," Jon said. "Coded, of course, but then there was a separate file with names and dates and background information on the kids. We've been waiting a long time for this break, so we did everything strictly by the book. The warrants to seize the computers are as clean as a whistle. Once we had our hands on the hard drives, it took a whiz kid from IT about as long to locate the files as it takes me to pick out a pair of socks in the morning."

"Jon," I said, "I couldn't be happier for you, and for the kids this creep—Wyman—didn't get to yet. And now he won't. I hope a jury sends him away until he's got a beard down to his knees. And we both know how welcome child molesters are in the prison population. But I still don't know why you're calling me about this."

Jon said, "Lots of the photos are of kids he'd already gotten to. Those are the ones we'll need to testify, while a very expensive defense lawyer tries to break them down. But others were of boys he was…keeping track of."

My mouth was suddenly very dry. I swallowed, and said, "What are you telling me?"

"There are three photos," Jon said, "taken with a telephoto lens. A boy in his mid-teens. Good looking, black hair, olive skin. In the closest picture he's wearing a red jacket and you can see his face pretty clearly."

"Luke," I said.

"The code says LJP. But the other file has more information. Name, school, relatives. It all matches."

In my head I could hear Eliot Wyman mocking me, in his urbane manner. *Perhaps someday the younger generation.* I would have killed him with my bare hands.

"Luke is my nephew," I said. I was surprised at how calm I sounded. "My brother Ned's son. Jon, I need to know something. You talked about some of these boys having to testify. Is there even the slightest chance that Luke could be one of them?"

"That shouldn't be anything for you to worry about," Jon said. "The photos of your nephew aren't in any way compromising, and believe me, we have plenty that are. I talked to a buddy of mine who's right in the middle of this investigation, and he doesn't see a thing to be gained by dragging in boys who were being watched, but hadn't been approached."

"And you're sure there's no danger to Luke?"

"Nell, we have the guy. He's out of his dirty business."

"I can't thank you enough," I said.

"No big deal." He paused, then said, "I didn't do myself proud when you were out here looking for answers about your brother. So when I saw the name "Prentice" in Wyman's files I made it my business to see if there was a connection."

I said, "It means more to me than you can know that you called."

"No problem," Jon said. "Well, you take care of yourself now. And say hello to that lieutenant for me."

"I will. Thank you again."

We hung up, and out of habit I reached for my calendar to match the call with a case. But of course there wasn't one. This was a personal and private matter, and with this phone call Luke and I could really put his father's death behind us. I took a moment to wish peace to Ned and our parents, resting beneath the same stone under a small willow Luke and I had planted.

I moved the calendar aside and positioned my computer mouse instead. I pointed it to WRITE.

Dear Luke,

I'm coming to get you as planned the day classes end, but I want to come this weekend, too. No big deal - just want to see you. What can I bring you? Love, Aunt Nell.

CHAPTER TWENTY SEVEN

My nephew goes to school in western Massachusetts, in a small town that plays to the nostalgia a lot of people seem to have for a past that never really existed. In the seven months since Luke and I found each other I had made the drive a number of times, either by myself or with Luke, in the range of weather New England can offer. It seemed to me that the fourth Sunday in May, a week prior to the Memorial Day weekend, would probably offer exemplary weather and pre-tourism traffic. I was right about the latter, but the former assumption proved to be a good reminder of why I don't hang out my shingle as a soothsayer.

I could hear the downpour before I even opened my eyes Sunday morning. I reached over to turn on the radio by my bed—Woody squeaked happily from the hall, *You're up, you're up*—but I pretended not to hear him as I tuned in WBZ. The weatherman, sounding as hyped as if a Category Five hurricane was headed our way, assured me that the wind and rain—"heavy at times"—would continue all day, with the possibility of coastal flooding. It seemed that my old friend Zeus Nepheleigereta, Zeus who gathers the storm clouds, was having a high old time sending this Spring surprise down from Olympus.

Realizing I was going to need extra driving time if I was to be at Ashfield in time to take Luke to lunch, I got out of bed and fed Woody on my way into the shower. I then combined the usually leisurely activities of coffee and breakfast, cat petting, and letting my hair dry so as to be ready to leave the house by eight.

"Tonight you can have some of my dinner," I shamelessly bribed Woody, to get him to stop looking at me with those orphan eyes. "Just settle yourself on my bed and nap away this rainy day the same way I'd be doing if it weren't for getting to see Luke."

The excitable weatherman had counseled me to carry an umbrella, but as soon as I stepped outside I realized how useless such protection would have been. The rain was battering sideways, driven by a briny-smelling wind. I knew I was smelling Boston Harbor, not the most pristine body of water, but the odor was exhilarating. The sounding sea—promising voyages and adventures as it had for millennia.

By the time I reached my car, parked several blocks away, my Gore-Tex jacket was drenched, and I had to loosen the hood to have a quick look around for marauding traffic before ducking into my car. I took a minute to peel off my soaked jacket and toss it into the back seat, then awkwardly exchanged my rain boots for shoes before pulling on my seat belt and starting the car. Every glass surface immediately fogged. When did the design of defrosters change so they do the opposite of what they're supposed to? I turned on the air conditioner, and the stormy world outside my car appeared, from the bottom of the windows up.

If the weather wasn't cooperating at least the traffic was, moving steadily and even according to traffic rules toward the Pike. I took the On ramp, eased carefully into the center lane before reaching for the travel mug of coffee I'd brought, and was on my way. For some reason, maybe the combination of the unseasonable weather and the fact that I was driving to a boys' school, I thought of Housman. He'd described a day just like this, in England, a century ago.

The doors clap to, the pane is blind with showers—
Pass me the can, lad—there's an end of May.

The speaker laments that the rain has ruined a season "of our little store," and is unconsoled by the probability that May twelve months hence will probably be fine.

O aye, but then we shall be twenty-four.

Did people still read Housman? I remembered how his poems—minor, in literary history's judgment—had stirred me as an impressionable teenager, and hoped so.

The rain began to abate as I left the Pike and followed the now-familiar back roads to Ashfield. All around me trees were a rich, wet green, as if I were driving through a park. I looked at my dashboard clock as I signaled to turn into the school grounds—11:30, perfect. I had eaten a light breakfast and hoped Luke would want to go to lunch at a nearby diner long on comfort food. Would I like macaroni and cheese? Grilled ham and cheese with chicken noodle soup? My mouth watered, and I swallowed. First the social niceties, then I'd be free to think about feeding my face.

"Ms. Prentice," said the housemother as I stepped into the entrance hallway of Luke's dorm, having thoroughly wiped my feet and shaken out my damp jacket. "What a day for ducks."

"Ms. Hansen," I said. "It's nice to see you. It's actually a lot worse in Boston than here."

"Oh, Boston..." she said vaguely, as if waving away the notion of some exotic locale like Alexandria from which I might have come by chariot. "Luke's in his room—why don't you go right on in."

I knocked on Luke's door and heard his voice—was it slightly deeper in just these few months?—tell me to come in. He was sitting cross-legged on his bed, using his laptop, which he closed as I came into the room. Good manners, or was he on some site he didn't want Aunt Nell to see?

That is *so* none of your business, I told myself. Aloud, I said, "Hi, honey."

"Hi, Aunt Nell." He stood, gangly and graceful at the same time, and I took the opportunity to hug him. He squeezed back and quickly let go. I knew I wouldn't have gotten even that smidgen of affection if his roommate had been there, and felt grateful.

"So," I said, standing in the small room, casting for conversation starters. "How are you? How are exams going?"

"OK. Geometry was a bi...really hard. I think I did OK in English and French."

I was hoping he might decide to take Latin for his third and fourth year, but I was still way too new in the role of *in loco parentis* to think of pressing my own choices on him. And what persuasive arguments would I use? It was doubtful whether he cared that Latin would enrich his own language for him, or even that he'd get to read some of the world's greatest literature in the original. For a moment I pondered a cash bribe, then thought what Roman moralists like Cato would think of such a gesture and abandoned my nefarious idea.

"Great," I enthused. "I'm sure you did fine."

"Scott's probably flunking out."

Whatever I had expected Luke to say in response to my confidence in him, it wasn't that. My senses went on alert. Was the subject of Scott, of flunking out, something my nephew wanted to talk about?

"Have I met Scott?" I said. Luke shook his head. I persisted, "Is he a friend of yours?"

"Sort of," Luke said. "We have history and art together."

"And he thinks he's flunking out?"

"He sort of knows he is. He skips class and doesn't study and stuff."

I wanted very much to know what "and stuff" was, but I didn't, as the mobile expression has it, go there. I said, "That's too bad. I wonder if he's said anything to his parents."

Luke looked at me. Those eyes—my own hazel color, but set off by his golden skin and long lashes. The girls were going to be chasing him way too soon for my liking, which is to say any time before he's thirty. "They're divorced. Scott's stepmother hates him."

"Oh, I doubt…" I began, then stopped. What did I know? Poor Scott—even if he only thought his father's new wife hated him it had to be hard. But I was more concerned with Luke, and with why he had brought this up.

"Are there other kids?" I asked. "Stepbrothers or sisters?"

Luke rolled his eyes. "She's having a kid. Scott's supposed to think it's going to be his brother or sister. As if."

I felt some sympathy for all concerned, not least the forthcoming baby. But I thought I might be getting a signal about what was concerning Luke. I took a breath and mentally invoked my wise friend Martha to address the question that was really being asked.

"It's different with us," I said. "The Prentices. You, Woody and me. If you get married someday"—he made a face—"your wife might keep her maiden name but you'll still be Luke Prentice. And if I ever married again I sure wouldn't be having any babies, and I'd keep our name—your father's and your grandparents' name—and anybody with that name would come first in my life. Right up there with my hypothetical husband"

I couldn't read his expression, but I felt I had done my best, whether I'd addressed what was going on in his mind or not, and now I needed to quit while I was, maybe, ahead. I said, "Would you like to invite Scott to lunch with us?"

Luke shook his head. "He can't leave the school grounds. Because of his grades."

"Oh. Well, I brought plenty of Milanos. Maybe he'll want some next time you see him."

Understandably, Luke didn't respond to my implication that Sugar Fixes Everything. I said, "So—lunch for the two of us. Want to go to Kenny's?"

"OK," Luke said. He picked up a denim jacket from the floor and pulled it on, then stood waiting for me to go out of the room ahead of him. When we were outside—the rain barely a mist now, carrying the smell of the flowerbeds we were passing—I said, "I would have liked to meet Scott, but I'm also glad it's just the two of us. I have something to tell you that is strictly between Prentices."

CHAPTER TWENTY EIGHT

The first time I met Luke we went to a diner that had hot dogs and burgers and every other variation of the kind of adolescent food that makes my heart beat faster and my cholesterol soar. I knew that the town also had an inn with starched tablecloths, fresh flowers, and no doubt dainty portions, but Luke and I were Prentices. If all-American comfort food is on offer, please let us through.

The menu in Kenny's was unchanged, the wipe-clean (or not) laminated menus ready for our perusal. Luke and I both decided on bacon cheeseburgers, his with onion rings and mine with French fries. When the food came Luke ate the fried batter off the only vegetable in sight and left the onions. Had I been his mother, I would probably have felt compelled to say, "That's not how you eat onion rings." I didn't even set an example by helping myself to an onion, since the batter is my favorite part, too.

I let Luke eat in peace, and did so myself, without interrogating him about school. His reports came to me, and he was doing fine. In fact, I was surprised and grateful that such a smart kid didn't think to ask for a car as a reward for the academic achievement I so prized. (In my mind I was already sitting in the shade of Harvard Yard, dressed to kill, listening to him deliver his valedictorian speech.)

When Luke was eating his sundae—where did he put it all?—and I was drinking coffee, I said to him, "I told you I had something to tell you that's just between us. Do you want to hear about it now, or wait until we're back at school?"

"Now's OK." He sounded cautious.

"Well," I said, and immediately stalled by finishing my coffee and signaling the waitress for a refill. Then I added creamer and Sweet 'N Low as if the fate of nations depended on the precise proportions, and finally took a sip.

"You remember my trip to California," I said to Luke. "My two trips."

Even as I said it I realized I probably should have begun this conversation outside, or in Luke's room. Kenny's was crowded, and conversations were definitely not private—what if Luke said something about Eliot Wyman and the sculpture I'd returned to him? But Luke just nodded, slightly.

"When I came back the first time I told you that both the men who..." I paused to choose my words with care... "were involved with your father were ...gone."

Luke was stirring his sundae. The chocolate and vanilla ice cream was melting into swirls, dyed red by the cherry.

"Then after our trip to Maine, after you helped me find what I was looking for, I went back to California. I'm pretty sure you were disappointed in me that time."

"You gave the treasure back," he said. His voice was flat, and any hope I had that he would contradict me about being disappointed was dashed. The "treasure" he was referring to was a bust of Alexander on Bucephalus, exquisite and, as it turned out, deadly. My brother, this boy's father, had died for it.

"We've talked about why I had to do that. But anyway, here's the other news I just found out about, and wanted to tell you first. The man I took the treasure back to—he's been arrested."

Luke's finely-shaped eyebrows went up. Those weren't the Prentice features—they must be from his mother's side.

"I'd like to be able to tell you that I had something to do with it, but I didn't. The law caught up with him for other things. It looks as if he's going to be spending a long time in prison."

"Finished with that?" It was the waitress. Luke nodded, and she removed the liquefied sundae. When she was out of earshot I said, " It's over, Luke. This man got to have the treasure for a little while, but it's not going to do him any good."

Luke was looking down at the table, tracing a circle in a dab of spilled ice cream. "Where's the treasure now?" he said.

"I don't know, honey."

"As long as it brought him bad luck," Luke said.

CHAPTER TWENTY NINE

With classes ended at Hathorne College and my interviews conducted, I had no reason to visit the college or call Alec Benson unless I had news. Which I did not, with less than two weeks until the Hathorne graduation. The invitation to Harry Marcus's wedding arrived, understated, with no doves or trailing silver ribbons, and I resolved to look forward to that even as I wracked my brain for other avenues of investigation that might lead to the missing manuscript. I made certain my blue and lavender summer dress was dry cleaned and still fit me, and purchased a tasteful clock as a wedding present. The stern Marcus Aurelius (*Every hour make up your mind sturdily and as a Roman to do what you have in hand*) would probably approve my industry and organization, if not my results in my paying case.

In a way, I was even further from success than when I took the job. I'd been comfortable with my assumption that the theft would turn out to be an inside job—someone on the Hathorne staff wanting to make trouble for Professor Benson or Alice. That scenario no longer seemed likely after my interviews. My mind had turned next to a profit motive—could someone have taken the manuscript to make money by selling it? Again, such a theory didn't hold up. The manuscript was certainly valuable, but it wasn't priceless, like the art treasures sometimes heisted from museums, including some in Boston. Those thefts had two possible motives: a ransom for the art object's return, or an illicit sale to a billionaire for his private enjoyment. And somehow I didn't think the object of my search was going to turn up in an Allston pawnshop, among the hocked jewelry and landscape paintings and beat-up musical instruments. More than anything else I worried about environment, shuddering at the thought of the Lucretius moldering in somebody's damp basement.

I kept that unfortunate image at bay as much as possible by working hard in my office, so that by Thursday I was not only caught up, but had made a start on organizing the tax records I would soon need for my quarterly filing. Harry was getting married at noon on Friday, so I was taking that day off, making a short local trip on a day when the roads leading out of Boston were likely to be jammed with holiday travelers.

When I woke up on Friday and listened to the weather report, I was happy that last Sunday's stormy weather had been one manifestation of Spring in New England, and today was an altogether different one. It was sixty-five degrees at eight in the morning, not expected to top seventy, dry and sunny. Harry and—I thought for a moment—Stephanie had a fine day on which to begin their lives together.

After breakfast, I opened the windows. Woody came running to choose the sunniest one from which to chatter territorially at the pigeons landing on the ledge. After fifteen minutes or so of being ignored by the fluttering birds, he tucked his head under a paw and went to sleep.

The doorbell startled us both. I was reading (an activity Marcus Aurelius would definitely not approve. *Away, away with books*, he chides more than once) and got up quickly to buzz Tom in. He had on a blue suit with an apple-green tie I'd bought him, and was carrying flowers.

"Are those for me?" I asked. Tom held the delicate bouquet out to me—violets, of all romantic things.

"Sure thing. Happy Memorial Day weekend."

I kissed him before taking the flowers. "Nobody's ever given me violets for Memorial Day. Thank you, sir."

I looked around for a vase, settling on a blue plastic mug, which I filled with water and set in the sink. Tom didn't look at all surprised at this inartistic way of arranging flowers—we were both familiar with Woody's compulsive need to sniff, nibble and ultimately capsize a vase of cut flowers. At least this way the mess would be contained in the sink, and there wouldn't be any glass for him to cut himself on. While the flower eater himself greeted Tom, I took the opportunity to close and lock the windows and collect my purse and the wedding present, in its pastel brocade wrapping. The store where I'd bought the clock had gift-wrapped it for me, so it was eminently presentable.

We were going in Tom's car—he had an actual parking lot behind his apartment building, so giving up a parking space wasn't the major hassle it was in my neighborhood. I sat back and enjoyed being a passenger, on my way to share the happiness Harry Marcus and his children deserved. I had downloaded and studied the directions, and would be able to jump right in if Tom's GPS guided us into a dead-end street, or even a dumpster, as I have personally seen occur.

The white fence outside the house we arrived at, with no need for my help, had white draped sashing and white balloons. Half a dozen cars were pulled up on the grass, and Tom parked expertly behind the furthest one and came around to open my door. Hand in hand we walked through an arched gate and into the yard, where Harry and a smiling woman in a rose-colored suit were greeting their guests.

"Nell!" Harry said, reaching to shake my hand. I ignored it and kissed him.

"Congratulations, Harry. I'm so glad you invited me."

"Thank you!" he said, still blushing from my kiss. "Nell, I'd like you to meet Stephanie."

I was meeting Harry's bride-to-be for the first time and thought a handshake might be appropriate here, but Stephanie held out her arms and hugged me to her. When she stood back, beaming, I saw that she had a kind face, alight with happiness, and that Harry's face held the same joy.

"We're so glad you could come," Stephanie said. She looked past me, and I belatedly remembered my manners.

"Sorry—this is Tom." Handshakes and congratulations, then Stephanie said, "Harry's told me, Nell, what a good friend you are to him and the boys."

"They're around here somewhere," Harry said, and just then I heard *Mrs. Prentice!* in two excited voices. I turned to see Monroe sprinting toward me, with Madison right behind. Oh my God—they were wearing dove-gray Eton suits with short pants. They had white rosebuds on their jackets, to match Harry's boutonniere. I flung out my arms as wide as I could and caught them both.

"Mrs. Prentice!" Madison said, pulling back so he could look at me. "We're ring bearers."

"Except," his brother chimed in, "we can't have the rings 'til right when Daddy and Mrs. Lovell need them."

Mrs. Lovell. I remembered Harry's telling me that their mother had insisted these boys not call adults by their first names, and felt admiration that Harry and presumably Stephanie respected her wishes.

"Mrs. Lovell made cheese sandwiches," Madison informed me.

"With *no* pickles," said Monroe.

From behind me Stephanie said, with a smile in her voice, "We also have fancier refreshments, but I did make the boys' favorite. It's their day, too."

Other guests were arriving, so Tom and I walked toward the seating area, where several of the white folding chairs were already occupied. We chose seats in the back row and sat back to talk quietly and, in my case, eavesdrop on the conversations around us.

A lovely lady.
So good to the boys.
…happy for all of them.

And from down in front, an observation by a tiny, white-haired woman in peacock blue.

"Don't they look like they're in love?"

I did a mental calculation. If the lady in blue was ninety, as she certainly appeared to be, she would have been born around the time of the First World War. Had she seen a sweetheart off to the Second World War, a son or daughter to a later conflict? All that she must have seen, and here she was, happy to enjoy a Spring wedding in the twenty-first century.

The empty seats were filling up, which must mean that the ceremony was about to begin. As the guests settled in I noticed Harry's sister-in-law Lisa in the front row, with Monroe and Madison on either side of her. She waved, and the boys, following her gaze, waved as vigorously as if they hadn't seen me in ages.

Recorded classical music began playing as a man in a clerical collar walked between the rows of chairs. I looked at the back of Madison's neatly combed head and wondered if the music sounded any different to someone with perfect pitch. Next came Harry, who exchanged a big smile with the minister as he turned to face his guests. The music stopped—there was an expectant flutter—and the first notes of the Wedding March issued from the unseen speakers.

Stephanie came slowly down the aisle in her rose-pink suit. She was carrying white roses, and looked like a queen. Her smile was for Harry, and his for her, while the rest of us did our teary best.

The ceremony was brief. The ritual phrases and responses, the "I will's" that, following the bit about anyone having reason to object, I always hold my breath for. Then Lisa whispered to her nephews and lifted two pillows she must have had in her lap. Each of the boys took one and let Lisa steer them the few steps to where Harry and Stephanie were waiting. Harry whispered something to Madison before taking the ring from his pillow and placing it on Stephanie's finger. She then took the ring Monroe had, smiling at him, and reached for Harry's hand to put it on. The minister said a few more ritual words and then pronounced them husband and wife. I fumbled in my purse for more tissues, saw that Tom was holding out a pale green handkerchief for me, and took it. Then I laughed along with everybody else as Madison broke the solemnity of the moment, in a very audible stage whisper.

"Can we have the sandwiches now?" he said.

Tom and I stayed for the refreshments and the cake cutting, with the boys given the pieces right after the bride's and groom's. As people began to leave, stopping on their way to congratulate the newly married couple, Tom and I joined the short line.

"Harry," I said as the woman ahead of us moved aside, "Stephanie. I'm so happy for you—for your perfect day."

"We'll have you over for dinner," Stephanie said, in a warm voice that said the invitation was genuine, not just social. "Both of you, of course..." Before I could reply to that, Tom said, "Thank you. I'd like to see you both again, and the boys." My knight in shining manners. I gave him a grateful and probably a bit proprietary look.

"So that's your friend Harry," Tom said as we were driving back to my place, where I was imagining a cat nap as soon as I changed out of my wedding finery and brushed my frosting glazed teeth. I had had two glasses of champagne and was feeling pleasantly buzzed as we drew up to my front door.

"From what you've told me," Tom went on, "he deserves something good like this."

"Oh, he does," I said. "He and the boys, and Stephanie. Wasn't she nice?"

Tom double parked in front of my building and I got awkwardly out of the car, clutching a slinky purse and a wrapped piece of wedding cake, teetering on my heels.

"Back soon," Tom said, "depending on how far I have to go to find a parking space." He had a Newton Police placard which he never used unless he was on duty. I can't imagine that I'd have such scruples if such a prize ever came legitimately into my hands.

"I'll wait up for you," I said, "as long as it's no more than fifteen minutes." I passed my tongue over my sugary teeth and called after him as he pulled into the street, "We were really smart to get you your own toothbrush for here."

CHAPTER THIRTY

om and I were invited to a noon cookout on Saturday at his mother's. We spent a quiet morning at my place, lingering over a light breakfast and second cups of coffee. "One thing you can always count on," Tom said. "You won't leave my mother's house hungry." Sheila Kramer had insisted we need bring nothing but ourselves, but I had asked Tom to stop on the way back from Harry's wedding so I could buy hyacinths, named for one of the many golden youths unlucky enough to catch the eye of Apollo. The flowers were in my bedroom, safe from Woody, who was alternating between Tom's lap and mine, preceded by our alerting each other, "Here he comes—watch your coffee."

In addition to a toothbrush in my bathroom, Tom now kept a few clothes in my hall closet, next to the rarely-deployed vacuum cleaner. (My apartment just doesn't look natural when it's been whisked completely clean of cat hair.) He put on jeans and a white button-down shirt, along with a comfortable-looking navy sweater for the predicted cooler weather. "I'd wear the gray sweater you gave me at Christmas," he said, "but I know I'd get barbecue sauce on it."

It was just as well. Tom's mother and I had become friends—I was the first person she'd called when Tom had a heart attack last Fall—but I was going to be meeting Tom's brother and sisters and their families for the first time. There would be quite enough curiosity about our relationship without the Kramers deducing that Tom and I had spent Christmas together at a motel in Maine.

While Tom, dressed and ready to go in five minutes, sat back down with Woody and the newspaper I went to my bedroom to choose an outfit. Why didn't I own any of those cropped pants other women always looked so good in? Was there time to run out and buy a pair? I looked at my alarm clock—10:30. I settled on my best jeans, the ones with a bit of stretch fabric in the waist, and a blouse with pink and blue vertical stripes. The nursery colors reminded me that one of Tom's sisters was pregnant—at least she wasn't likely to be in a size two bikini. After a critical appraisal of how the color went with the blouse, I added a cotton sweater Martha had knit for me in a rich shade of deep rose.

"Do I look all right?" I asked Tom as I came out of the bedroom, carrying the flowers. He put down his paper and smiled.

"You'll be the prettiest woman there. I'll have to stay close to you so Patrick doesn't try to steal you." Patrick was Tom's brother, never married, but, according to Tom, one for the ladies. I felt flattered and much more at ease, which was no doubt what kind-hearted Tom intended.

"Ready?" he asked. He got up carefully, with Woody waiting until he could no longer defy gravity before jumping from his lap. We walked in the sunshine to where he had parked the car, and I got in beside him, happily anticipating hot dogs and chips and potato salad. Oh, yes—and meeting his family.

When Tom pulled up in front of his mother's house it looked as if there were dozens of people in the yard, even though there were only three cars parked in the driveway. Tom came around to open my door—his mother, who was waving to us over the head of a child she was holding, had taught him such courtesies. Sheila crossed the yard to us and said, "Nell, I'm so glad you could make it. I'll hug you as soon as I put this big boy down. Ryan, this is Mrs. Prentice. Can you say hello?"

Ryan buried his blonde head in his grandmother's neck. *Mrs. Prentice.* Would the Kramer clan think Tom had taken up with a married woman? Or a divorced one? My newest silly worry was put to rest when a dark-haired woman came up to Sheila and said, "Let me take him, Mom." The little boy averted his face as his grandmother handed him to her daughter and said, "Frannie, this is Tom's friend Nell."

"Pleased to meet you, Nell," Frannie said, reaching to shake my hand. Tom's sister had a few freckles and a resemblance to him. "Tom, it's about time." She gave him a hug, around her clinging child, and said, "Come meet everybody. Ryan is mine, and the two girls over there..."

I was introduced to the girls, and Frannie's husband Jeff, a big man with the fair coloring of his youngest. Then came Maura, in a maternity dress, who hugged me before turning to Tom and echoing her sister's opinion. "Finally you let us meet Nell. If it weren't for Sheila telling us all about your great lady friend we'd all be thinking you made her up. Now where did Patrick get to...? Oh, here he comes."

I looked toward the house and saw a John Kennedy, Jr. lookalike coming toward us. Same height and presence, same dark hair and eyes, a Celtic lord set down in a Boston suburb. Behind him, catching up with him as he moved across the yard with casual grace, was a blonde girl I decided must be the oldest niece. Patrick stopped next to Maura and slung an arm around her. "What about it, kid—a girl this time?" He turned his sexy smile on me. "Maura and Steve have three boys—we'd like to see some pink in the nursery this time around."

"Pay no attention to him," Maura said. "Having no babies of his own..." ("At least none that I know of," Patrick said, and ducked the slap Maura aimed at his hand) "...he doesn't get it that healthy is all that matters. Healthy baby, and as short a time as possible for Mother in the delivery room. Nell, this is our brother Patrick and his friend Kelly."

His... I saw my mistake and must have blushed, because Patrick gave me an amused and knowing smile. I managed not to stammer as I said, "It's nice to meet you, Patrick. And you, Kelly." I wondered if she spelled it with a "i" on the end. Patrick's friend, who up close still looked like a teenager, was wearing short white shorts, a tiny purple T-shirt, and flip flops with rhinestones on them. Tom could have prepared me for this, but then I remembered he had implied I'd give this Junior Aphrodite a run for her money, so I decided I had the better half of the Kramer brothers. I took Tom's hand—Kelly was now draped sinuously along her man—just as Sheila called, "The young natives are getting restless. Everybody please come eat."

It turned out that Patrick was more than just a very pretty face—he also flipped a mean cheeseburger, grilling one-handed as Kelly clung to him, flirting with his two giggling nieces as they waited for their hot dogs. When my turn came I accepted a juicy burger and a big scoop of Maura's potato salad. As I went to join Maura, who was sitting on a lawn chair with her plate balanced on the swell of her middle, I heard Patrick say, "Babe? Try one of these heavenly Kramer burgers?"

"Patrick!" Kelly said, sounding aghast, "I told you—I brought my yogurt."

Her waist was maybe twenty inches around. I caught myself rolling my eyes and stopped, but not before Maura noticed. She grinned as I took the chair next to her, and said in a lowered voice, "They last about six months. Every one of them looks like the Barbie dolls Jen and Nicky play with." Patrick had moved away from the grill and was deep in conversation with Kelly, so Maura raised her voice to a more normal level. "We used to think Patrick would get tired of the hookups and breakups and want to settle down, but at this point I doubt he's going to change."

I thought I knew where this conversation was going, and said, "I suppose it gets a lot harder to change when you're older."

"Tom's different," Maura said. So much for my hopes that I'd forestalled any inquiry into Tom's and my relationship. "He's a one-woman man. One *real* woman—not one off the Mattel assembly line."

I laughed, though not without a twinge of sympathy for Kelly. I wondered how long she'd been with Celtic Ken. Just then, to my relief, I saw Tom heading toward us with his plate.

"Ladies," he said. "May I join you?"

"Yes!" I said, and then hoped my eager tone hadn't hurt Maura's feelings. She said to her brother, "Nell and I have been getting acquainted. I was just saying nice things about you to her."

"I'll ask Nell later if that's really true. But how are you doing? When is my niece due?"

After the meal there was coffee and ice cream—the harlequin variety that kids love, as do I. Maybe Ben and Jerry, my main men when it comes to ice cream production, could come up with a seasonal flavor such as Memorial Day Marshmallow. Putting aside thoughts of exotic flavors, I accepted a block of the brown, white, and pink ice cream as happily as the children did—except for Ryan, who screwed up his face and said, "Don't like that!" Frannie took Ryan on her lap and began feeding him spoonfuls of ice cream from her own plate, which changed his tune. His face was soon as ice cream besmirched as the faces of the other kids. I felt surreptitiously around my mouth to be sure I was eating like a grownup. Kelly was having black coffee for dessert—I actually thought I saw her reading the Sweet 'N Low packet to make sure it didn't contain so much as half a calorie.

We grownups were in a large circle of chairs, with the kids at a picnic table that was their size, and there seemed to be no further interest in Tom and me as a couple, or at least none expressed aloud.

I thought such reticence might be a result of Sheila Kramer's having taught her sons and daughters good manners. It was also possible that Sheila, being a direct lady, had issued a stern warning against prying. Whatever the reason, I felt relaxed and included in the family party.

By midafternoon the sky had clouded over and there was a chill in the air. Tom's sisters began calling to their children to put on sweaters and jackets, which the kids resisted, and when Ryan began to fret and cry the families began packing up to go home. Tom and I let them get their cars out before making our goodbyes to Sheila—Patrick and Kelly had disappeared back inside the house—and telling her what a nice time we'd had.

"Take some leftovers," Sheila said, reminding me of Martha, who always provisions me for my brief journey home as if I were crossing the continent. "Unless," Sheila said to me, "you already have enough food back at your place for the rest of the weekend."

No doubt about it—that was a plural "you." I reflected that if Tom and I ever were to get married, I'd be related to this lady. A good deal. I said to Sheila, "Maybe just a couple of those nice hamburger buns if there are any left. I've got cold cuts to make sandwiches for…" I paused, "…our supper."

Sheila hurried off, looking happy, and returned with a bulging bag. "There's potato salad," she said, "and plenty of the rolls, and a cut-up hot dog for Woody. And"—this added casually—"some fresh ground coffee for the morning."

When Tom and I were in the car I said, "Your mother knows how to drop a hint."

"Always has," Tom said. "Plus, she has excellent taste—she can see what a catch I've made." He was quiet for a minute, returning the squeeze I'd given his hand. "You know, Nell, I've sometimes been embarrassed by the way Patrick acts—the world's longest midlife crisis, with no ending in sight. But today was the first time I felt sorry for him."

"Sorry?" I repeated, thinking of Kelly's nubile figure and adoring manner. "Why would you feel sorry for Patrick?"

"Good old sibling rivalry," Tom admitted. "He's used to getting all the attention for showing up with one pretty girl after another. But today I stole his thunder by introducing my family to a beautiful woman who I happen to be going home with."

I could feel how big my smile was. "Mr. Kramer," I said, "if you weren't already coming home with me, you certainly would be after that remark."

CHAPTER THIRTY ONE

Tom had switched hours with a colleague so he could go to Harry's wedding with me, so he was working Sunday, which happened to be one short week before the Hathorne graduation. Tom left early, saying he'd get breakfast on his way to work, and I eventually got up to make coffee and grill some cheddar cheese on one of the leftover rolls. I could think of nothing but the hours ticking away toward the ceremony Mrs. Greenberg would be attending. At noon, unable to bear the thought of obsessing for the rest of the day over the likely repercussions if I didn't locate the manuscript, I called Alec Benson at home.

"Professor Benson," I said when he answered, "It's Nell Prentice. I hope I'm not disturbing you." I also hoped he wasn't looking disappointed at his end of the line—he must have known that if I'd found the Lucretius a call with that good news would be anything but a disturbance.

"Not at all," he said courteously. "I'm working on translating a lovely bit of Tibullus. Perhaps you would be so kind as to take a look at it when I have a first draft."

I could not let this man down—a distinguished Hesiod scholar who was treating me like a colleague. I said, "I'd be very honored and flattered. The reason I'm calling is that, naturally, I've been thinking about how quickly graduation and the award ceremony is coming up, and, well, I wanted to run something by you."

The idea I had, my only idea, was that I talk to Mrs. Greenberg— try to sound her out, without giving anything away, about how she might react if her husband's gift were not on display next week. Not nearly as good as actually locating the manuscript, but maybe I could buy a little time to keep looking. I could say that in spite of excellent preservation techniques the manuscript needed cleaning. Or that it had been mistakenly sent on loan to a museum and was on its way back, but not in time for graduation. I'd think of something—Herodotus, Father of Lies, had always stood by me.

"I don't have a better idea," Professor Benson said, an endorsement of sorts. "I think your idea is certainly worth a try. You may not find Henrietta at home, though—she has friends who are similarly—well-off—and gets quite a few invitations to vacation homes."

"I'll call first," I said. "And of course I won't bother her if she chooses not to talk to me. Could you give me directions to the house along with the phone number—if I can't reach her I may drive by and leave a note in the mailbox."

I knew perfectly well what Professor Benson fortunately didn't. Once I got to the house, if Henrietta Greenberg was at home I was going to have a conversation with her. Time was getting way too short. I did show a shred of good faith after we hung up by calling Mrs. Greenberg's number, but I got the answering machine. I didn't leave a message but instead got in my car and drove to the Beacon Hill address I'd been given. As I drove up the steep hill I actually saw an aristocratic-looking white haired man out walking with a little girl in frilly organdy and a small boy in a sailor suit. Shades of the nineteenth century, when my own forebears were probably working as parlor maids and bootblacks in these houses, if they weren't risking life and limb building the railroads.

The Greenberg house had a handsome brass plate with its street number, and a polished knocker on the mahogany front door. I lifted the knocker and rapped with it, wondering if today's version of a parlor maid might appear to see who was calling on My Lady. But the door was opened by Mrs. Greenberg, who looked at me with no sign of recognition.

"Mrs. Greenberg," I said, "Please excuse my coming by without talking to you first. I did call, but I got the answering machine and took a chance that you might be home. We met in Professor Benson's office—I'm Nell Prentice. Could I talk to you for just a few minutes?"

"Actually," she said, "this isn't a good time. I'm just back from visiting friends on Nantucket. And I'm invited out again shortly."

I wondered why, with the difficulties of getting to and from Nantucket on Memorial Day weekend, she would come home on Sunday instead of staying until after the holiday, when the people who had to be back at work would be gone. Also, I noticed that she was wearing a robe and slippers. If she were just arriving back, wouldn't she be in her Talbots weekend casuals, with a color-coordinated summer blazer?

"I promise not to take up too much of your time." I smiled at her, and played what I thought was a pretty cagey card. "Professor Benson thinks the world of you—he'd never forgive me if he heard I was making a nuisance of myself."

"Dear Alec," she said with a fond expression I hoped to benefit from. A look of recognition, if not fondness, came into her eyes. "You're the one studying at the state school."

I gave her a big smile that I hoped would conceal my annoyance at her elitism. "You have a good memory. In fact"—I kept smiling—"you told me there would be a classical manuscript on display at graduation. You said you hoped I could attend, to see your husband's gift."

"Did I?"

I sensed that she was regretting getting into a conversation with me and was about to remind me she was on her way out. This was the moment I was either going to botch this assignment or get her to see reason when, as I was probably going to have to do, I told her the manuscript was missing.

"Mrs. Greenberg, I am a classicist as Dr. Benson said. But I'm also a private investigator working for Dr. Benson. There's something I need to talk with you about."

She stood in the doorway for another minute before saying, "Come in, then. But just for a few minutes."

What I had to tell her wasn't going to take very long—her reaction would be the unpredictable part. She opened the door and I followed her inside, where the furnishings looked opulent, though by no means overdone. Then, in a transformation I've seen before, her manner thawed some once I was actually in her house. She said, "May I offer you tea? As I said, I have to leave shortly, but my Clayton wouldn't want me having a guest in his house without providing some refreshment."

A chance to snoop around unobserved? For that she could bring me Lapsang Oolong, which to me tastes like the water from a boiled dinner. I said, "Thank you. Tea would be lovely." As soon as she was out of the room I began scoping everything out, hoping I looked like a connoisseur of fine furnishings rather than an intrusive P.I.

As I looked from paintings in gold frames to objets d'art on ornate stands I realized that not everything seemed to be in its place. There were darker areas on the walls where paintings seemed to have been recently removed, and stands holding nothing. A large area of the hardwood floor looked as if a rug had covered it, and there were noticeable gaps in the floor to ceiling bookshelves. Interesting.

Mrs. Greenberg came back into the room carrying a tray with tinkling cups and saucers and an embossed silver cream and sugar set. She poured the tea and held out a china plate of paper thin cookies, of which I accepted a ladylike portion.

"What delicious tea," I said, sipping from my flowered cup. It tasted like ordinary Lipton, which was fine with me. "And these cookies are just heavenly. Did you make them yourself?"

"I have a wonderful cook. Her pastries are the envy of my friends." She hadn't taken a cookie, or touched her tea. "Since I'm out so much for the holiday weekend I insisted she take time off. Ms. Prentice, I wish we could relax over our little *soiree* here, but since I *am* going out..."

"Absolutely," I said. "This is such a beautiful house." I sipped at my tea and nibbled a feather light cookie. "Of course I've never had the pleasure of being here before, but I can't help noticing the spaces on the walls and the floor. Do you have a lot of your possessions in storage?"

This was an extremely mannerless question, but Mrs. Greenberg did not seem to take it as such. My strong feeling was that she was being evasive—sometimes when that's the case the person who's been asked a rude question is so busy thinking up the next bob and weave that it never occurs to her to say: none of your business.

"They're out to be cleaned," She was looking down at her hands, and I noticed something else was missing—the rings she'd been wearing in Alec Benson's office. "The rugs and art work are very valuable— I've had them sent out to specialists who know how to preserve fine furnishings."

"Goodness," I said brightly, "The books, too? I'm impressed! I never seem to get around to even dusting my books, though I know I should."

She didn't answer that, and I decided to take my chance before she could come up with any further unlikely explanations for the missing items.

"Mrs. Greenberg," I said, "I'm a friend and admirer of Professor Benson. He is a friend and admirer of you. I'm also, as I said, a private investigator. I may be in a position to help you, but only if you tell me what's going on here."

She did look at me then. Her face was flushed, and I thought I saw tears in her eyes. She said, "I'm so ashamed of what has happened. If my friends ever found out… I've had to stop accepting invitations, or having anyone here."

"Friends can surprise us by how understanding they are," I said. "And your friends are certainly not going to hear anything from me. Suppose you just begin at the beginning and tell me what's happened."

For the next half hour I sat holding my empty tea cup, not wanting any distraction to interrupt Henrietta Greenberg's story of what had taken place with her nephew Henry.

"My sister's boy. Josephine and her husband named him for me. Clayton and I had daughters, and Henry became like a son to us. Then when Clayton died Henry just stepped in to take care of everything. Clayton had always taken care of our finances, and I would have been lost without Henry."

She drew a breath. "The first time the bank called, I was quite sharp with them. I told them my nephew had power of attorney, and I had complete confidence in him to manage my investments as he saw fit." Another breath, with a slight shudder to it. "By the time I realized how much money was missing, it would have been a criminal matter. I couldn't bear the thought of that." Henrietta Greenberg seemed to collect herself, and when she spoke next it was in a calmer voice.

"Since you're working for Alec, Ms. Prentice, you are probably aware that in addition to the manuscript my husband left Hathorne a generous endowment. Which I can no longer afford. I needed a reason to stop the endowment, with no one finding out why."

I waited to be sure she had finished speaking. Then I said quietly, "And the reason you came up with was to have the Lucretius go missing."

She nodded, just barely. "I was invited to dinner at Alec and Tanya's on a Saturday night last month. They both think of me as a friend, not just another rich donor. I slipped into Alec's study on my way to the powder room and took his set of department keys from his desk drawer. On my way home I stopped at the college and removed the manuscript. The next day I invited Tanya to lunch at a new restaurant I said I'd been wanting to try. When we got back to her house I returned the keys to where I'd found them."

So now I knew why the manuscript was taken, but I still needed an answer to the question I asked next.

"Mrs. Greenberg, where is the manuscript?"

My question seemed to take her by surprise, as if the answer should have been obvious. "Why, here. Clayton had a room on the second floor properly humidified for some books and other items that needed a controlled environment. I would never let any harm come to something my husband treasured so much."

Her expression was quite composed now, as if she had shed a burden. "I suppose you'd like to see Clayton's gift," she said.

CHAPTER THIRTY TWO

I put down my empty cup and got up to follow her. She led the way up a curving staircase to a large study at the back of the house. Here, nothing appeared to be missing. I wouldn't have been surprised if not even the smallest item had been moved from the position Clayton Greenberg left it in. His wife crossed the room and turned the key in what looked like a closet door. Behind the door was a large space, about twelve by twelve. I stepped in after her as she removed a dark cloth and turned on a recessed light. She moved to one side, and I had a full view of the manuscript.

The photograph I had seen had not done the artwork justice. It glowed in tones of gold and sand and yellow, with marble black backing the poet's name and *liber primus*. Trees and cliffs and mountains and water were background for columns and a mantel, on top of which cherubs steadied a dark red A—the first letter of Aeneadum, which begins the poem. It was magnificent.

I let out the breath I had drawn in at the sight of the beautiful work. "Mrs. Greenberg," I said. "I can only imagine how proud your husband would be at the care you've taken of this."

"Thank you," She had tears in her eyes, and one fell as she whispered, "I don't know how I'll ever face Alec and Tanya again."

I said, "That's one thing you don't have to worry about. Professor Benson hasn't said anything to his wife and he's not about to. When he hears about the situation you were put in he'll have nothing but sympathy. You said it yourself—he considers you a friend."

She said without looking at me, " I still can't bear the thought of calling him. Could you…will you see that it's returned?"

"Yes," I said. "But before I do that there's something I want to talk to you about. Perhaps we could have another cup of tea?"

We went back to the living room, and I waited for her to serve the tea and begin sipping hers before I broached my idea.

"Mrs. Greenberg, I think you need to tell people what your nephew did to you." Her lips parted in alarm, and I said, "I know—he's your family, and you feel embarrassed that you trusted him. but that's all you did—trusted someone close to you, who wasn't worthy of it. You have nothing to be embarrassed about. And there's something else."

She was listening to me, waiting. I said, "You must have friends in a similar position to yours. On their own, with money their husbands left to keep them secure. If your nephew could do a thing like this to you, he's entirely capable of victimizing your friends in the same way. Or women you don't know, who could lose everything."

"You think I should go to the police."

"I'd start with your lawyer," I said. "Tell him or her everything, and let the lawyer make contact with your nephew. It's possible this can be resolved without criminal charges, if your nephew makes full restitution to you and promises to have absolutely nothing to do with your finances in the future. If there are already other victims, of course that would be different. But either way, Mrs. Greenberg, you'd have every reason to be proud of yourself. You'd have done something courageous."

"Proud of myself," she said. She set her cup on the coffee table and met my eyes. "I know this is the right thing to do, but it will still be difficult. Do you think I could call on you if need be?"

"Yes." I reached for my purse and took a business card from the outside pocket. "I'm writing my home number on the back. Call me anytime."

She took the card, then looked at me. "This would mean I could continue the endowment."

Homer says *The hearts of the brave can be healed.* I'm sure he'd understand that sometimes before that can happen, you have to take out a few greedy cowards.

We packed the Lucretius together, she with a skill I guessed came from years of overseeing the transport of fragile objects. When we were finished I had a bubble-wrapped rectangle to carry to my car by its cord loop. Mrs. Greenberg stood in her doorway as I carefully laid the package on the passenger seat and went around to the other side. She waved and went back inside, and I took out my cell phone.

"Professor Benson? It's Nell Prentice. How goes the Tibullus?"

"In truth, I am sitting in my garden, courting inspiration. One must do justice to such a poet."

"I've just been to see Mrs. Greenberg, and I wondered if you could meet me at your office. I realize you may have guests, or be going out…"

"Tibullus is my only guest at the moment, and he will wait. Shall we say half an hour?"

I waited in my car in the nearly empty parking lot until I saw him drive up, then got out of the car with the package.

"I believe this belongs to you," I said, holding it out to him as he reached me.

"What is…" he said, and then, "Oh, my. You've found it."

"Could we talk inside?" I said. He nodded, and we walked to the Classics entrance. In his office I laid the package on his desk and we sat in the visitors' chairs as I told him what I had just learned.

"Mrs. Greenberg has agreed to take action to stop her nephew once and for all," I said. "She realizes this could become public and an embarrassment for her, but I got the sense that she's tougher than she looks. And I told her I'd help in any way I can.

"There's one other thing, Professor. She's worried sick that she'll lose your friendship. She told me she didn't know how she could ever face you or your wife."

"I see." He looked at me. "First, Ms. Prentice, I want to say that I can't thank you enough for what you've accomplished. It was a lucky day for me and my Department when you decided to come to my lecture— even though no one at Hathorne will ever know how close we came to losing the endowment. I'll tell Alice the manuscript is back and that will be the end of it." He stood, and gestured to the package on his desk. "I'll put this in the storage room just as it is—when I come in on Tuesday I'll unpack it properly. You and I need to leave together so I can lock up, and I don't want to keep you. I just need to make one phone call."

He carried the package to the room it had been taken from and stepped inside with it. After he locked the door he went to his desk and picked up the phone.

"Henrietta? It's Alec. We'll be seeing you next week at graduation, of course, and I know this is short notice, but I wondered if you could come to supper tonight? I'll make my crab cakes, and I know Tanya wants you to see what she's been doing in the garden. Six o'clock? It will be just the three of us."

He hung up and took his keys from the desk. I didn't have the words to express how touched I was by his simple humanity, but once again Marcus Aurelius had them for me.

Put an end to this discussion of a good man, and be one.

As soon as I got home I called Tom. "I know this isn't really your type of outing, but do you remember that lecture I went to? Well, the professor who spoke teaches at Hathorne and he found my office number and called me to say there's going to be a manuscript on display at graduation—something I'd really love to see. It's this Saturday—can you go with me?"

Tom said, "I'd better say yes. I don't want you meeting up with some guy who speaks Latin and taking that trip to Italy with him instead of me."

"Not going to happen. Thank you."

I hung up and thought that it wasn't every day that, in the space of an hour, I got to have a conversation with not one but two good men.

CHAPTER THIRTY THREE

Hathorne's colors, blue and white, were everywhere on graduation day. The fifth of June had started out overcast, but by late morning the only clouds left were puffy summer ones, in a deep blue sky. Since Hathorne was an urban campus, the graduation was held on the grounds of an impressive white house the college owned north of the city. Students in blue and white gowns posed with their families, proud parents snapping picture after picture with cameras the size of playing cards.

"Just think," I said to Tom. "In two years Luke will be the one graduating. I wonder where he'll want to go to college. I feel as if I just met him and now he's almost grown up."

Tom squeezed my hand. "And right after that the Marcus boys will be out of college and running for the Senate. Relax, Nell. There's plenty of time."

He was right. Time to enjoy this unique day that wouldn't come again. "Come on," I said. "Let's find a place to sit. I'm glad there's a tent—I didn't think to wear a hat the way the Queen always does."

Alec Benson and I had agreed that it was best not to reveal any special connection between us. He would be sitting on the platform with the other department heads, and since his wife and I had never met she wouldn't recognize me. Alice of course would, and did. She was coming toward us beaming, wearing a yellow dress.

"Ms. Prentice! It's so nice to see you again. Isn't it a beautiful day for the graduation?"

I turned to Tom. "Alice is secretary to the head of the Classics department. I attended one of her boss's lectures. Alice, this is my friend Tom."

Alice got the hint—she and I barely knew each other. Her skin reddened slightly, and she said, "I'm glad to meet you, Tom." Her new-found expertise in detective work rose to the occasion. "Ms. Prentice, since you're interested in the Classics, there's a wonderful manuscript on display. A benefactor donated it to the college."

I smiled at her. "I'd love to see it. Can you point me in the right direction?"

Tom and I stood in the line of guests waiting to view the Lucretius. When it was our turn, I was as impressed at the manuscript's beauty in daylight as I had been seeing it in a windowless room. A kind of shadow box protected the manuscript on its easel from direct sun, but it seemed to glow with its own light. I said to Tom, "Have you ever seen anything like this?"

"It's really something," he said. "I know you can tell me all about it, but there are people waiting, so I guess we should save that for home."

I had a last look at the beautiful treasure before Tom and I moved on to the tent where chairs were set up. We were almost to the Unreserved section when he said, "You were looking at that manuscript as if you'd done it yourself."

I turned to look into his brown eyes. They were as guileless as Woody's can be when he knows something and wants to communicate to me how smart he is. I kissed Tom on the cheek.

"I think I'll keep you. What about here, on the aisle."

The graduation speeches were standard fare, filled with references to "beginnings" and "journeys" and "the future." The valedictorian had a shading of acne and one earring. But like every graduation I've ever attended, it was special because of the graduates themselves. So young, asserting their individuality in alterations to their caps and gowns—a peace sign, hand-sketched stars, the greeting HI MOM. The world would take them where it would, but for today, it was all theirs.

The last few graduates were up on the platform, about to join their class in the final ritual of their college days. A girl shook the President's hand and took her diploma, then the girl behind her, and finally Samantha Jane Wilson. A few rows from the front a small group cheered and whistled, causing Samantha Jane to duck her head and grin. When she had crossed the platform and walked down the few steps the graduates all faced the President.

"Ladies and gentlemen, family and friends," he said, "I give you the Hathorne College class of 2005."

Off came the mortarboards—were they still called that?—with their shifted tassels, and up in the air they went, blue as cornflowers. The guests were on their feet, clapping, and I wished everyone there a life that would always hold some of their present happiness.

Tom and I walked past tearful girls hugging each other, small siblings released to run and spin on the grass, and the clicking of photos that would, probably in some digital version of the family album, recall this day. Other people were also leaving, and Tom said, "Shall we let them all get out first? We could wait here." He pointed to a white stone bench under a flowering tree, and I walked ahead of him to it.

"Thank you for coming with me," I said. "I enjoy everything more when I can do it with you." Tom was watching the cars pull out of their spaces—about all that was visible of the driver of a white sedan was a large flowered hat. He turned to me and said, "I feel the same way. You're the part of my life that was missing, and I didn't even know it."

We sat quietly, joined in a comfortable silence. Music carried faintly from the white mansion, where I knew the celebratory reception was being held. Tom said, "Nell."

I looked at him. He said, "I want to have this always. The good times like today, but the bad times, too, when they come. Will you marry me?"

My mind stilled, then filled up with a whirlwind of considerations. *I'd have to keep working. I wanted to keep my name. Whatever else changed, I needed to be there for Luke.*

The flight of time. Sometimes the only thing we can do is let it lift us up and carry us with it.

"Yes," I said.

Tom laughed, and got up to take a few steps away from me. He brushed a hand over his eyes, and I realized he had been prepared that I might say no. I said, "I want everybody to know. Can we call Luke and Martha tonight?"

He turned, with such a huge smile that he looked as young as the kids who had just graduated. "What about my mother?" he said. "She only asks me once a day."

I felt myself smiling as widely as he was. "Well, let's not keep her waiting then. Here…"

I reached into my purse and pulled out the little cell phone that, most of the time, I want nothing to do with. Today, it would carry our fine news. I held it high, gave my wrist a twist, and let it go. It sailed through the air, bright as Mercury, and Tom reached out and caught it.